Praise for

THE STONES
CRY OUT

"Okuizumi's understated prose, eloquently translated, is the perfect vehicle for a sensibility trau-
matized by history."
—*The New York Times Book Review*

"This eloquent, sorrowful, marvelously translated
novel is a meditation on the ravages of war, the
persistence of violence on the human soul and
the incredible bravery that (perhaps) each of us
shows when we try to mask that violence, or
bury it, or turn it into something 'productive.'"
—*The Washington Post*

"An eerie and engrossing novel . . . As polished
as any pebble in Manase's sample case."
—*The Boston Globe*

"A lyrical, riveting study of obsession . . . Okuizumi is a natural storyteller, his deceptively simple, low-key style is magnetizing."
—*Publishers Weekly*

HIKARU OKUIZUMI

THE
STONES
CRY
OUT

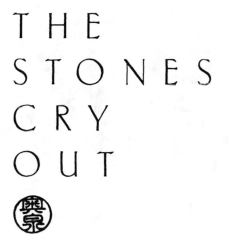

Translated from
the Japanese by
James Westerhoven

A HARVEST BOOK
HARCOURT, INC.
Orlando   Austin   New York   San Diego   London

Ishi no raireki by Hikaru Okuizumi
©1993 by Hikaru Okuizumi
Original Japanese edition published by Bungeishunju Ltd.
English translation rights arranged with Hikaru Okuizumi through
Writers House Inc./Japan Foreign-Rights Centre

English translation copyright © 1999 by James N. Westerhoven

Library of Congress Cataloging-in-Publication Data
Okuizumi, Hikaru, 1956–
[Ishi no raireki.   English]
The stones cry out/Hikaru Okuizumi; translated from
the Japanese by James Westerhoven. — 1st ed.
p.   cm.
ISBN 978-0-15-100365-5
ISBN 978-0-15-601183-9 (pbk.)
I. Westerhoven, James.   II. Title.
PL858.K845I8413   1999
895.6'35—dc21   98-14434

Text set in Weiss
Designed by Linda Lockowitz
Printed in the United States of America
First Harvest edition 2000
M L K J I H G

He answered,
I tell you, if these were silent,
the very stones would cry out.

LUKE 19:40

CHAPTER ONE

EVEN THE SMALLEST stone in a riverbed has the entire history of the universe inscribed upon it. The reason Tsuyoshi Manase became a fanatic collector of stones can be traced back to words spoken to him by a dying man during the Second World War, in mid-December 1944, in a cave in the middle of the tropical forest above the Bay of Carigara in northern Leyte.

The man was wasted by malnutrition and amoebic dysentery, and his face resembled a skeleton of wires covered with parchment. Only his eyes moved, restlessly. These eyes he now fixed on Manase. With his emaciated fleshless fingers that seemed more like roots to Manase, the man picked up a stone from the ground.

This should be classified as green chert, he said in a magisterial tone, as if he were addressing a group of students. The cave was formed when bedrock from the Paleozoic era rose to the surface and was eroded by the sea. Later, during the Quaternary era, the sea withdrew and left the cave in the midst of jungle. Thus the walls around them were probably full of fossilized marine organisms. If you were to examine this little piece of rock under a microscope, the man informed Manase, you would be sure to find radiolarians and the like. His lecture continued more or less as follows:

"You normally don't pay much attention to the stones you see by the side of the road, do you? Oh, perhaps if they're stones you can use for your garden, or your house, say, but in general you don't give much thought to them. You just think of them as meaningless objects scattered in the mountains, rivers, and fields. Even if they're in the way, it doesn't occur to you that they might be worth picking up and studying. Well, you're wrong, you know. Even the most ordinary pebble has the history of this heavenly body we call earth written on it. For instance, do you know how rocks are formed? Rocks are formed when red-hot magma cools and solidifies; rock erodes under the influence of wind and weather on the surface of the earth. That's how you get stones. Stones are eventually ground into sand, sand into soil; then stones and sand and soil are carried away by streams and settle on the bottom of lakes, fens, or the sea, where they once again harden into rock. That rock crumbles and changes back into stones and sand and soil, or it may be pushed deep beneath the surface of the earth and, under the influence of heat and tremendous pressure, reborn as rock, in all shapes and sizes; or sometimes it melts into magma and returns to its origins. The form of minerals is never static, not for a second; on the contrary, it undergoes constant change. All matter is part of an unending cycle. You know of course that even the continents actually move, though at an imperceptibly slow pace.

"What I'm trying to say is, the tiny pebble that you might happen to pick up during a walk is a cross-section of a drama that began some five billion years ago, in a place that would later come to be called the solar system—a cloud of gas drifting idly through space, growing denser and denser until after countless eons it finally gave birth to this planet. That little pebble is a condensed history of the universe that keeps the eternal cycle of matter locked in its ephemeral form."

Manase had spent a year and a half as a prisoner of war in the camp at Calanban. Only after he was released and had settled in the village where his mother and father had fled from the war had he begun to dwell on the words the man had spoken as he lay stretched out on his bed of rocks. What immediately struck Manase was not the words he had heard in that cave with its evil stench, but the maggots. As a person's flesh and fat waste away, the eyes begin protruding from the skull, which explains why a starving person's eyes seem unnaturally large. If a skeleton had eyes, they would be nothing if not conspicuous. Since the eyes of people weak with sickness generally lie motionless in their sockets, Manase thought it strange that this man's pupils moved relentlessly as he talked. When Manase looked more closely, he saw maggots. The man's eyeballs were swarming with them. Not that maggots were a rare sight in the cave—all around lay dozens of rotting corpses with maggots crawling beneath their skin, and Manase himself had a sore on his knee filled with them—but this was the first time he had seen maggots squirm in the eyes of a breathing, talking human being.

But what impressed Manase most was the intimate, fatherly tone in which the man addressed him. No one had spoken to Manase in such a friendly way from the moment he had been drafted in early January 1943, when he joined the regiment in Yamanashi, until he reached the front, near the Pacific. This man was not only a lance corporal and therefore Manase's superior, but more important a veteran several years his senior. That such a man would suddenly address him so warmly threw Manase into a panic. At first he did not realize the man was talking to him; when he did, he was so dumbfounded he could not keep his eyes fixed on the middle distance as military discipline required, but instead let them wander. Manase lay down beside the man and closed his eyes. The delirious lance corporal continued talking into the darkness of the cave long after Manase had turned on his side, facing away from him.

On the front, sleep often comes suddenly, in the form of deep coma, yet the words stayed with Manase. That he heard them still was less peculiar than stories he had heard in the camp, such as the vision of a lady in ancient court dress beckoning unceasingly from between the dark waves, or the jellyfish creature the size of a whale that a fighter pilot had seen floating above the clouds. Compared to such apparitions, a talking soldier hardly seemed reason to ponder the strangeness of memory. Perhaps the lance corporal's words had made their deep impression because they contrasted so poignantly with the incessant drone of airplanes and the roar of cannon on the front. Soon, Manase's recollections of the war began to fade, and all that remained fresh in his memory was the lance corporal's sermon about the stone.

Later, when Manase began to play around with stones, those words assumed a distinct shape and lodged themselves in his heart. Whenever someone asked how he began collecting stones, Manase would let his memory drift back to the time spent inside the cave on Leyte. He was never able to find the right words, and because he was not eloquent, he would reply only with a modest smile from his small, deep-set eyes and hope that would answer the question.

Manase's father had once run a secondhand bookstore in the Kanda area of Tokyo. When

the winds of war began to blow cold on everyone's skin, despite rosy newspaper dispatches,
people began whispering that before long the
homeland itself might be bombed, he had been
one of the first to close shop. He took his family
to the town of Chichibu, in the mountains
northwest of Tokyo, where he had distant relatives. They led a refugees' existence in a storehouse rented from a farmer, but soon the
owner's family died and Manase's father was
asked to buy the farm and the surrounding land.
That is how they moved into the main house.

By the time Manase was repatriated to Chichibu in the spring of 1946, his father had died
of a chronic heart ailment. His mother and two
elder sisters still lived on the property, in the
shadow of enormous holm oaks and camphor
trees. Manase went to the printer's shop in Ueno
where he had worked before the war, but found
a burnt-out wasteland, and the boss who had always looked after him had disappeared. Manase
saw little choice but to return to Chichibu,
where he helped his sisters grow vegetables in
the garden and started a secondhand book business with the piles of books his father had
brought with him from the old shop in Kanda
and put away in the storehouse. The son loaded

them on a handcart and peddled them door-to-door.

Although he did not anticipate much demand in a small town like Chichibu, he soon was doing a brisk business, so once a month he took as many books and vegetables as he could carry to Tokyo, where, thanks to his father's reputation, he was able to buy the new magazines that had slowly begun to appear after the war. Now that people were able to feed themselves again, they snapped up any scrap of paper with print on it. The prewar Iwanami pocket editions sold quickly. English and American literature—products of the "Anglo-Saxon devils" and therefore safely hidden in the storehouse during the war—brought astonishingly high prices. Once word spread that Manase had stocks of classic detective novels (a hobby of his father's), orders from readers near and far poured in like rain. Manase left a handwritten catalog with a friendly bookseller in Kanda, and the mountain of books—which his mother used to say was "only in the way and would never make a single penny"—melted before his eyes.

With this money Manase opened a store in Chichibu. He divided the narrow space—one half for secondhand books, the other for new editions—and after only half a year was able to expand and start a lending service. His two sisters were excellent seamstresses, in both the Western and Japanese styles, and they worked also. They had a good reputation in the neighborhood, and soon became so busy they had to hire the neighbor's daughter as part-time help, and the wide hall with the stamped dirt floor at the entrance to the farm began to resemble a workshop. The Manase family no longer had to worry whether they could support themselves.

About this time Manase began collecting stones. Because his house was in the western outskirts, in the foothills of the mountains surrounding the Chichibu Basin, he always rode his bicycle to work. Every day he would stop at the bridge over the Arakawa, walk down to the river, and smoke a cigarette on its bank. Morning and evening, in a daily ritual, he stared out over Mount Buko and the other peaks of the rugged mountain range, and one summer morning, already drenched with sweat from the heat typical of a basin, Manase took off his shoes to cool his feet in the river and noticed a small brown stone glistening in the water. It shone so prettily that he picked it up. Its gloss appeared to be caused by tiny grains embedded in the groundmass, and when it caught the sunlight, it sparkled even more dazzlingly in the palm of his hand.

After finishing work in the evening, he went home, took a bath, ate dinner, and only then did he put the morning's discovery on the desk. But the stone had dried and lost its luster and was now no more than a dull piece of gravel. Manase was disappointed, but the next day he picked up more stones. He remembered he had a goldfish bowl somewhere; he filled it with water, and when the stones sank to the bottom, the effect was very pleasing. From then on he never failed to collect a few stones every day, paying particular attention to color and pattern, until he had five or six small water tanks filled with stones.

He discovered an old book in his store that described a method for polishing them. Ordinarily, stones are placed in a rotating cylinder filled with a mixture of water and emery powder, but because stones found in riverbeds have been polished naturally and sparkle so brightly, Manase decided only to add the finishing touches. He discovered that to bring out the full luster he must use a chemical substance with a strange-sounding name: cerium oxide. Unsure where he could find cerium oxide, he tried ordinary carpenter's varnish, with unexpectedly good results. He checked one department store after another and came back with metal polish and all sorts of varnish, and from that time his daily routine involved locking himself up in his study and working on his stones. Before long he wanted more than just to line them up and admire their beauty. Now he wanted a collection.

First he had to memorize their names and then categorize them by color. Because Dr. Kazunosuke Masutomi's *Mineralogical Handbook with Illustrations in Natural Colors* would not be published until 1955, a good Japanese manual did not exist, but as a bookseller Manase had no problem finding illustrated geological books for children; he collected as many as possible. Staring at the rows of rocks on his desk did not get him far, though. All stones are different in shape, depending on how they were broken. There must be a way to arrange them by color, but a single type of stone could have many shades of color. Even the presence of extremely small crystallized particles of metallic elements such as potassium, iron, or sodium seemed to make a difference. Granite, for example, could be white or veined with red, bright but also

11

dark. Granite with big crystals was not such a problem, but if he could not distinguish the small crystals with a magnifying glass, he had no choice but to give up. "Inspection of a polished section under a polarizing microscope makes it possible to determine the nature of the rock-forming minerals and thus to arrive at a definitive classification" was the blunt, heartless advice he found in one of his books.

Bewildered but unwilling to give up, his notebook always within reach, and armed only with the eyes and fingers his parents had given him, Manase treated stones with hydrochloric acid and with magnets, broke them and scratched them and sniffed them and licked them, until after about half a year he could identify the most common rocks simply by holding them in his hand. By this time the desk in his storehouse was covered with rows of stones, each with its own label. Moreover, he had the good fortune to become acquainted with the geography teacher of the local high school, who often visited his shop, so he now had a specialist he could consult. And when this teacher helped him obtain the standard set of fifty minerals that had so often made his mouth water, his classification work progressed with amazing speed.

The stones he found in riverbeds no longer seemed satisfactory. Each week on his day off he would hike into the Chichibu Mountains, a topographical map in hand and a hammer in his belt, and walk from outcrop to outcrop. He still made many mistakes—this was specialized fieldwork—but he enjoyed himself tremendously and seldom left a single stone unturned; often his canvas bags became too heavy to lift. As he gained experience, and became expert with his hammer and chisel, he was able to go to the mountains and tap out a specimen of exactly the required size along the grain of a rock.

To his delight he discovered that Chichibu was a mecca for geologists. The Paleozoic, the Mesozoic, the Cenozoic—each era was represented in magnificent strata: sediments of igneous rock, of course, but metamorphic and contact metamorphic rocks, too, were distributed over a wide area, starting with the crystalline schist around Nagatoro. Rare ores and fossils were also plentiful, and one might almost say that people living in the foothills had a treasure trove lying in their fields. The specialists had discovered Chichibu early, and meticulous geological maps provided an invaluable reference for the amateur scientist.

Manase began his own collection of specimens with the tentative goal of fifty different kinds of rock, which he deposited one by one in the box he had built with his own hands. Six months later, on the day his eldest son was born, Manase had all fifty stones; he immediately raised his goal to one hundred. That number proved to be high for Chichibu alone, so he used the New Year's season and the Bon holidays in August to explore the entire Kanto plain around Tokyo and even traveled as far as the island of Kyushu. What he could not find himself, he tried to get from mining companies. One midwinter day, this time just before the birth of his second son, he succeeded in buying from an acquaintance the siderolite he badly wanted for his collection, and when he slipped it into the last empty slot in his box, his collection of one hundred stones was complete.

If Manase ever felt like complaining, he did not have far to search for reasons, but at least he did not suffer from famine or fear of a sniper's bullets, and as his peaceful life continued, he was reminded only rarely of the things that had happened in the war. Only when he lay shivering in bed during one of his malaria attacks did the events on the front float like phantoms to the surface of his memory. And what his nightmares brought back to life, more than anything, was his terror of loneliness.

Alone in the green prison of jungle—ferns with cruel, hard leaves and grotesquely squirming vines jumped out at you from everywhere—it was enough to drive a woodsman out of his wits, let alone a boy who'd grown up in the quiet. outskirts of a big city. Such had been Manase's desperation as he wandered from hill to hill and from valley to valley looking for comrades after his malaria caused him to lose contact with his unit. It was in the chaotic days following the collapse of organized resistance by the Japanese army, while the Americans were hunting down its remnants in the forests. He would never forget the terror of those days. In his wanderings he had encountered many sick or wounded soldiers, groups of zombies, half conquered by death. If ordered, they would drag themselves a little farther, but in general their movements ceased before they had crossed the next hilltop, and then it was not long before their eyes, still staring into space, dried out in their sockets.

To avoid contact with the enemy, who controlled the roads, Manase had taken refuge in the roadless mountains, but during his wanderings he became isolated and his sense of direction was also gone. One horrible day and night of rambling aimlessly through the desolate jungle destroyed his remaining physical and mental resources. He had climbed down into a valley and was drinking water from a stream when suddenly he noticed a group of Japanese soldiers coming down the opposite slope. At that moment, he believed he would never feel happier in his life.

The group consisted of a dozen soldiers commanded by a captain. When their regimental headquarters were destroyed, this officer had gathered the surviving soldiers and organized them into a functioning unit. The captain, who appeared to be in his early thirties, made a strong impression on Manase. He was the highest-ranking officer Manase had ever addressed, and that might explain why he struck the barely twenty-year-old private as far older than his own father. The soldiers under his command jumped at his most trivial order with a vitality that surprised Manase, who had met nothing but living corpses in his wanderings.

"At this very moment the Japanese army is regrouping on the southern coast of Leyte and a fleet of transport ships is steaming south through the Bashi Channel between Formosa and Luzon. As soon as troops and arms have been amassed in sufficient concentrations, our Imperial Forces will launch their final battle," the captain reported.

Since his arrival on Leyte, Manase had been subjected endlessly to false propaganda, and by now he had lost all illusions. He understood very well that the captain's transport ships existed only in his mind, but the voice assuring him of their arrival sounded so clear and strong that his heart swelled in his chest and he felt a new hope surge within him—an ephemeral hope, perhaps, but enough to build a tower with, and if that tower was buttressed by powerful words and a powerful voice it might remain standing, even on loose sand. Moving toward a target with your comrades—compared to the despair of Manase's aimless wanderings in the nocturnal jungle—it certainly was hopeful even if you were moving toward your doom. More than once on his lonely way through the mountains Manase had toyed with the idea of taking a hand grenade out of his backpack and killing himself, but the thought of being blown to shreds of flesh on an anonymous spot in the middle of the forest without anyone finding out what had happened to him filled him with horror and made it impossible to pull the pin out of the safety. And because the most miserable, most painful aspect of his hopeless drifting was the uncertainty, Manase's immediate induction into the captain's unit restored his military peace of mind. He was able to relax: as long as he obeyed orders, he could continue his journey hallucinating. He had to work hard and was given no time to rest, but the work exhausted only his body. Whether he should turn left or right, climb up or down, crawl forward or walk backward, all those difficult decisions that could mean life or death were felt as if a heavy burden had been lifted from his shoulders. He no longer even had time to wonder what lay in store for him. But more than anything, the captain's voice issuing the orders was beautiful. It echoed in the pit of his stomach and seemed to pass through his body. It possessed a power that could be called magical; even the short, terse commands pleased the ear. If Manase heard that voice ordering him to charge, he would gladly throw himself into a curtain of machine-gun fire.

It was not only the voice. Among all those scorched faces indistinguishable from charcoal briquettes, the captain's pallor was conspicuous; Manase assumed he had the sort of skin that never tanned. And yet, even with his cap pulled so deeply over his handsome and (probably also naturally) beardless face that it almost disappeared under the peak, even with his uniform covered with mud, the captain never lost his authority. He possessed a power dangerous to resist. Although the soldiers seemed energetic enough, virtually all of them were sick or wounded, and because some of them were in bad shape, the group's ability to function depended on the willpower of its commanding officer. Some of the men seemed unlikely ever to stand again once they lay down; but as soon as the man with the eyes burning in the black shadow of his cap issued an order they jumped up and, like windup dolls, marched on, careful not to step out of line. Manase was no different. He lay spread-eagle on the ground; he could not move; it would be his death if he walked farther; but when the order to get up reached his ear, it was as if an enormous claw grabbed him by the intestines: all sensation seemed to leave his body, and to his amazement his body set itself in motion, jerking and hitching like an automaton. You could see the captain had graduated from the Military Academy, he thought admiringly. Such officers were different. The man radiated a supernatural authority that filled Manase with awe.

In the afternoon of the day Manase joined the unit, the soldiers discovered a deep cave in the middle of the jungle where they decided to bivouac. The cave was already occupied by Japanese soldiers, a bunch of half-dead stragglers who had abandoned all hope. Not only had they lost their rifles—despite perpetual warnings that a soldier's rifle was more precious than his life —but also some wore nothing but a sloppily tied loincloth below ribs that almost pierced the skin. Manase had seen more than his share of sick, dying soldiers and rotting corpses, but even he flinched at the stench and squalor in that hole. But here too the magical beauty of the captain's voice appeared irresistible: as soon as he stepped inside the cave and barked orders, human beings who had been covered with a carpet of flies and were being eaten by maggots jumped up as if they had just taken a hot bath, and diligently began cleaning up the filth around them, exactly as they had been told. Half of them did not obey orders...they were dead. Manase understood that even the captain could not bring them back to life, yet the unwilling-ness of these corpses to lift so much as a finger struck him as peculiarly obstinate.

Although there was some ventilation in the cave, the smoke from their cooking fires was not visible from the outside, so it was suited as a hiding place, and because there was fresh water nearby, it was not surprising so many Japanese soldiers had gathered here. Manase could not remember how much time he spent in this cave. Sometimes he thought it was less than two nights, sometimes he thought he stayed there more than a week. In the end his unit never resumed its march to the rendezvous on the south coast: the very first morning in the cave it appeared their indispensable captain had be-come hobbled by gangrene from a shrapnel wound in his left leg. His face turned ashen overnight, and he gathered all NCO's and sol-diers who could stand and told them his strat-egy. Because the mountains were swarming with the enemy, he explained, it was no longer pos-sible to reach the south coast, so they must use the cave as a base to fight their final battle. His final words permitted no dissent: "You're all go-ing to die here."

Occupy a strategic position and fight—it

was a splendid idea, but since they were low on ammunition and there were few soldiers who could walk on their own, it would be difficult to take the initiative and launch an attack. In other words, they would have to wait for the enemy to discover them before they could die in honor. They were, in fact, no different from the sick or injured soldiers inside the cave. Nevertheless, and despite his condition, their leader lost none of his willpower; under his command they maintained military discipline if not morale. They scoured the forest in search of food, for although officers and enlisted men had decided to die together, it is impossible to fight on an empty stomach—a literally empty stomach. How to stay alive until their last glorious sword fight became an important question for the unit in the cave, so Manase and a few other still reasonably fit soldiers decided to raid a nearby village. It did not turn out to be risky. Not only were the villages deserted, but they looked as if they had been attacked by locusts; everything edible had been eaten by Japanese soldiers. It seemed not even a blade of grass remained, but when they searched carefully they found some turnip greens, and a few lucky ones even found a gaunt chicken. Of course they also searched for food in the jungle—practically anything that moved, from snakes to lizards to insects, ended up boiled in mess tins or helmets.

The captain ate first, served by the soldier on duty, and what was left was divided among the salivating soldiers. The smell of cooking meat affected their famished bodies; their stomachs seemed to grow teeth and appeared ready to jump out of their mouths into the pan, and as soon as the steam began to curl upward, men long left for dead would crawl from the shadows of the rocks and stretch out their blackened fingers. Because the captain had forbidden food to any soldiers no longer able to fight, and because only soldiers who were still able to fight went foraging, the only ones who got to eat were those who could feed themselves. As long as you yourself were starving, you could not care less what happened to others, but as soon as you had food in your stomach, you began to care. You began to feel pity. If the captain wanted to fight one last battle, he as commanding officer had to give absolute priority to keeping the organization of the unit intact—in that he was absolutely correct. But if you saw those skeletal fingers coming at you, decency prevented you from kicking them away.

The captain issued an order: men who could no longer get up should end their own lives, immediately. Not one of the sick soldiers had enough physical or moral strength left to do it. The captain issued orders to kill them. You were going to die soon yourself, and if someone was in that much pain, it was actually a kindness to make it easier for him; the sick soldiers themselves were begging to be killed, so you grabbed your bayonet and prepared to end their suffering with one well-aimed thrust. At the last moment your courage melted away. You began to tremble. Boiling with rage, the captain struggled to his feet and limped toward the invalids, trailing his wounded leg, naked sword in hand, and one by one slit their throats. The soldiers who dragged the bodies away did not want to waste their remaining strength digging graves. "Please forgive us! Please forgive us!" they chanted each time they dumped a body in the forest. It sounded like an exorcism.

At the time he witnessed the massacre of the sick soldiers, the ruthlessness of the murderer seemed understandable. It was war. What fascinated him more than anything was the admirable expertise with which the captain put the edge of his sword lightly against the neck of a supine human being and, with a delicate, natural, but sure motion, cut the victim's carotid artery. No one screamed at the final moment, and, incredibly, there was not even any spurting of blood—at least not as Manase remembered. He could hardly believe that all those sick soldiers had died with a smile on their lips, but that was the undeniable image burnt into his memory.

The impression of the sword was overwhelming. Rifles, men, sky, everything was gray, drenched in blood and pus and filth—only the naked sword hanging from the captain's hand was bathed in a serene light, the steel of its blade clear as a rippling mountain stream. The death it announced was immediate and sweet. Each time the sword was unsheathed from its faded black leather scabbard, Manase followed it with his eyes until it had reached its mark, and at night, when the living and the dead lay sleeping on their bed of stone, he could not keep his eyes off the captain as he sat against the rock wall by the campfire, cleaning his sword of blood. He would pull the graceful blade out of its sheath, wipe the thin graceful blade carefully with a cloth, and hold the sword in front of his face, now colored red by the flames, study the edge with eyes—his eyes a fierce glitter in the shadow of his cap—then take up his cloth to wipe away another blemish. This process repeated itself until the blade became a mirror that flashed the light back into the captain's unblinking eyes. The shadow on the rock face trembled in the gathering wind, the play of light and dark intensified on the face of the man; only the naked blade remained motionless, the light it emitted seemed frozen.

Whenever Manase looked back on the events in the cave, this was the scene he remembered first. It seemed to him that the captain polished his sword at every free moment, not only at night. The figure of the captain, a bundle of willpower and tenacity despite his wound, instilled Manase with fear, as if the captain were a demon or damned soul, but the more he feared the captain, the more he felt attracted to him. Watching stealthily from his corner, Manase was unable to avert his eyes.

"Die!" the captain had screamed, and the death he had commanded seemed embedded in the bluish tinge of the sword tip. Manase tried to imagine what it must be like to die together with his commander, to fall under the fire of the recognizable enemy, hearing in his ears the voice that had ordained his death, spurred by the whistling of naked steel. He imagined himself in a field shrouded in a lilac haze, an infinitely tragic figure, the bullets piercing his flesh seemed to give more pleasure than pain. To shed tears because now he was about to die for the Great Cause he had heard so much about, at the same time yearning for a swift death—this was at least better than the hunger forcing you to dig out the maggots from your wounds and pop them in your mouth, or to cast an unconscious glance at the meaty part of a comrade's thigh.

Both at the front and in the prisoners' camp Manase had heard many rumors about cannibalism. Fortunately he had survived without having to witness such scenes, but his blood ran cold at the thought that they would not have surprised him. He could not say what he would have done if they had remained in the cave much longer and the captain had not been there to maintain discipline. However, once he was settled in his mother's house after the war, the physical memory of the hunger had faded, and although he looked upon the cave as a hell on earth, he no longer felt oppressed by the events that had taken place there. The only way he could recall his experiences was as a brief glance into a dark hole through a window, as a dream that he pondered while lying in bed in the morning.

He did not want to remember—Manase understood that very well. Even though he could taste his fear, he needed only to remind himself that he was lying on a soft mattress, not a cold bed of rocks, and the fear would retreat. Time fits together in a peculiar way: fortune and misfortune, pleasure and pain, all are exiled to the past to form a landscape in monochrome. It is a mystery—and a blessing.

Not long after he opened his bookstore in Chichibu, Manase married the daughter of a grape farmer from Yamanashi whom he had met through the pharmacist across the street. Because his two sisters had found husbands around the same time, Manase and his new wife lived with his mother, who was still mentally alert, but who had been hit by a motorcycle and was frequently confined to bed. The sun barely reached their home either in summer or winter, and they led a quiet life, but soon they had a child and that brought the house to life. The ancient room that housed the family altar turned out to be useful as a playroom, and before long its old-fashioned but extremely large and sturdy panel doors were covered with crayon scribbles.

"Your future husband doesn't drink or gamble and his only hobby is collecting stones, so you can see that he's serious and decent—none better," the pharmacist had told Manase's wife during the marriage negotiations, but all she could picture was an elderly man. Once married, she discovered that her husband was as serious and decent as the pharmacist had promised—but that his hobby was hardly normal. When she woke up in the morning she would find herself alone. Outside it would still be dark, too early for him to have left for work. There was nothing to do but get up and make breakfast. Eventually he would return, trudging down the mountain behind the house, with equipment dangling around his waist and a heavy-looking bag hanging from his shoulder. Once she asked what was in it. What came rolling out was nothing but rubble, not even fit to serve as weights on the lid of her pickle tub. Night was no different: after quickly eating his dinner he would retreat to the privacy of his storehouse, no doubt to play with his pebbles. Six months after the wedding he took her to the hot springs of Ikaho "because they hadn't had a honeymoon." Any illusion that she might soak in the baths or relax evaporated. All day they walked through the mountains, and every time her husband found a stone, he took his hammer and started tapping. She wished she had stayed home.

The pharmacist found it all very amusing. Yes, he laughed, you often heard of people whose hobbies had ruined them, but in this case...stones were free, so it wasn't costing a penny. Slowly the house filled with peculiar tools and instruments whose purposes taxed her imagination. Then one day Manase told her that an ordinary-looking piece of rock the size of a baby's head was worth at least one hundred thousand yen, which astonished her. The bookstore did an adequate if not brisk business. Their income increased steadily, and they were soon able to support Manase's hobby without having to economize. "My husband's heart may not be made entirely of stone," she sometimes complained, "but it might as well be, he's so boring. And the things he does—he'll drive me crazy!" This was really an indirect form of praise, for while it was true he did not talk much, he did not lack affection. And sometimes he would skillfully fashion a beautifully polished little stone into a delicate piece of jewelry, and although she told herself that it had not cost him anything, the gift pleased her. While she was busy raising their child, he never complained about the clothes she laid out for him, and he meekly ate everything she served. Then she was only too glad she had married a man who needed so little looking after. Her mother-in-law died in the fifth year of their marriage, and her death provided an opportunity to remodel the house. Manase's wife now ruled over the spacious, bright kitchen she had wanted for so long. She was given an electric rice cooker, a washing machine, and a refrigerator, and when she saw these electrical appliances, she knew—and her parents agreed—that she was risking divine punishment if she did not stop grumbling.

All the surrounding trees were cut down and replaced with a lawn, except for a small plot they continued to use as a vegetable garden. Now they lived in a house that can be seen in any big city: two stories, red tin roof, mortared walls, white-painted chicken-wire fence. The house looked out of place in the neighborhood. Only the ashlar storehouse, which stood in a corner of the property, preserved the memory of the old farm with its silkworms and vegetable beds. Despite frequent repairs the whitewash on the outside walls had peeled off, and because it had been installed later, naked electric wiring crawled like a centipede across the ceiling. But this storehouse was Manase's castle. The ground floor was used for storage space; half was filled with old books that could not fit in the store, half with apple crates full of unsorted stones. A ladder led to Manase's workroom, which looked like a chemistry lab, with several wooden desks covered with alcohol burners and mortars, microscopes, mysterious electrical appliances, piles of maps and reference works. The equipment was perhaps not of the highest quality, but the room made a splendid study. Manase's greatest pride were the racks he had built to display his stone collection, with specimens ranging in size from a chicken egg to an adult human head, each meticulously cleaned and labeled. The specimens were arranged under the three main categories—igneous, sedimentary, and metamorphic rocks—and then subcategories. Sedimentary rocks, for instance, were divided into clastic rocks, chemical deposits, and organic rocks. There was a special area for minerals such as cinnabar, pyrrhotite, or copper pyrite; there was another one for mineral crystals such as quartz, kaolinite, and amphibole; one rack had rows of jars filled with all kinds of sand; there was even a corner for fossils. Indeed it was a small museum. Yet Manase was not satisfied with the quality and quantity of his collection.

The geography teacher had taught Manase how to prepare sections, which gave him something to do with his stones besides collecting them. For this he needed an electric grinder, but since that was beyond his means the grinding had to be done by hand. At first this went well because he started with fusulinide limestone, which is relatively easy to handle. But that was as far as he got, for the stone must be split into very thin segments before the grinding process can be started. If he used a hammer or a chisel, the rock would crumble before he had acquired a piece of the desired size and thickness. Despite his stubborn wish to complete the entire process himself, Manase was forced to realize that until he found a cheap diamond stone saw, he must be content with visits to the local mining company to have his stones split into segments of the right size.

Once he had a thin piece of stone about one square inch, he would smooth it down with sandpaper or a file, polish it on an iron plate with a mixture of Carborundum and water, and then give the final touches with an even finer abrasive on a glass plate. After polishing one side, he would heat some Lakeside cement over an alcohol burner, glue the fragment on a glass slide, and then polish the other side. In theory, this should have resulted in a section whose mineral crystals in all their various hues appeared clearly in the lens of a polarizing microscope, but in fact the process was not that simple. It is extremely difficult to polish a section to absolute, perfect smoothness. If not done expertly, the surface remains irregular, and if you are not careful, the section will break. Gluing the section to the glass slide requires much skill, because it is very easy to get air bubbles in your cement, and bubbles mean you must start over. And every kind of rock is different. If a stone crumbles easily because the crystals are fragile, it may have to be treated with a binding agent to soften it up. Manase developed his own methods by experimenting with abrasives and softeners; he tried glycerine and kerosene instead of water, polished stones from early in the evening till late at night, and meanwhile he developed his own methods.

His name became known among lovers of

geology, and soon high schools and universities began asking for specimens from his collection. Sometimes complete strangers would send requests for a mineral assay. Such requests made Manase pursue his hobby with even greater enthusiasm. He also became increasingly interested in fossils. He investigated a Paleozoic stratum along the course of the Yokose River, and his distribution map of the fossils he found there proved so accurate that established experts in the field expressed admiration. From a Mesozoic outcrop on Mount Ryōkami he collected a magnificent ammonite, but the absolute zenith of his career as a do-it-yourself geologist was his discovery of the Paleoparadoxia.

While investigating an old quarry near Mount Shiroishi in the village of Ōtaki, Manase noticed the bones of a peculiar animal. Because he considered himself too inexperienced to handle fossils, he immediately contacted the geography teacher, and together they excavated fifty-two bone fragments in one month. A university in Tokyo identified them as the remains of a marine mammal called Paleoparadoxia that had lived during the Miocene; it was only the second time a virtually complete fossil skeleton had been discovered in Japan. This animal was later exhibited in the Prefectural Museum as "the Saitama Monster," and Manase shared the honor of its discovery with the geography teacher.

As his knowledge increased and he became more absorbed in geology, he was forced to think back to the Leyte cave and the lance corporal who had explained what was special about stones. The captain with the sword and, without any doubt, the lance corporal were the only people who had left an impression on Manase during the war. But whereas the captain's figure still seemed scorched onto his eyelids, Manase had only hazy memories of the lance corporal's face. He had already been in the cave when the group led by the captain arrived, so he probably was one of the survivors of the Kwantung army who had been transferred to the southern front in the fall of 1944. At first he had been fairly fit despite tropical dysentery, for he and Manase had foraged together. They were often separated from the others, so they spent much time in each other's company, but perhaps because of their continual fear of encountering American soldiers, Manase could not remember having a real conversation or even an opportunity to ask the other's name or where he was born. The

lance corporal opened his mouth only when absolutely necessary. The sick soldiers in the cave
seemed to trust him completely, and because the
lance corporal always seemed to know what he
was doing, Manase considered himself lucky to
have teamed up with him.

What sort of person was he? He appeared
fairly old, about the same age as the captain, but
that in itself was nothing special, for at the Leyte
front there were many veterans older than thirty.
Perhaps he seemed older because of his calm and
relaxed manner. He was not a student. The army
was filled with people from many walks of life,
so he might have been a scholar or the em-
ployee of a mining company. At any rate he was
someone who had done work requiring knowledge of geology—beyond that Manase did not
speculate. Later he was sorry he had not at least
delivered a lock of his hair to his family, but by
then the war had been over for some time.

The lance corporal's health deteriorated rapidly. Manase noticed how still he lay in his corner of the cave, and later he heard him talking
about stones in the dark, knowing that these
would probably be his last words. Manase had
seen it often: someone still strong enough to
burst into laughter one day would be still and

cold the next. So Manase's heart had gone numb and no longer reacted to human life or death. Too exhausted to take any interest in events not concerning him directly, Manase was unmoved by this man's impending death.

"Stones are not only formed by magma. There are also meteorites that come flying from outer space. But the major cause is organic activity. Along with water or ice, living organisms also play an important role in the erosion process, and then their bodies in turn change into stone. Surely you know that coal is nothing but fossilized wood from ancient trees. Limestone and chert consist of the compressed skeletons of tiny organisms that collected eons ago on the bottom of the sea. Even the calcium in our own bones will eventually change into stone and be made part of the mineral cycle. That is why the tiny pebble that you pick up from a riverbed, no matter how silent and alien, is in fact your very distant relative. That pebble in your hand tells the history of the world, and you too are a part of that history, and what you discover is the way you yourself will look in the future."

The lance corporal talked on. Surely his sudden outburst was an omen that the flame of his life was about to burn out. Manase may have purposely decided to sleep next to him, for though they had seldom talked during their acquaintance, he felt respect for the man and wanted to nurse him during his last moments. Manase's memory was blurred, for right about that time he had suffered another bout of malaria. It was still night when the lance corporal began his story, that much was certain, for Manase distinctly remembered looking toward the entrance of the cave and seeing nothing but an ink-black gloom. He had felt unbearably cold. (In the prison camp he had also had a few bad times: not even a thick layer of blankets could stop the chattering of his teeth brought on by fever.) He had wanted to warm himself but lacked the nerve to move toward the captain, who was keeping watch by the fire: he might have been polishing his sword, in which case Manase would not have dared invade that sacred space. He covered himself with as much as possible—dead soldiers' uniforms, anything serviceable—and as he lay shivering, the uninterrupted stream of words from the man next to him seemed distant, like a dream.

It must have been the dead of night when he woke with thirst. The lance corporal's voice had fallen silent. Manase looked at the fire and saw the captain talking to someone. There was a smile on his lips. Manase wondered who could be on such intimate terms with the captain, but he could not make out the person's face. Death himself? Manase mused without feeling fear. Is the captain dying too, and will that be the end of this camp? As the idea occurred to him, his mind turned cloudy again.

Next Manase remembered sitting in the sandy open space of a village square, surrounded by huts with raised floors and roofs thatched with palm leaves—a familiar background since his arrival in the Philippines. A number of Japanese soldiers were sitting near him, and a group of Filipinos stood around them in a wide circle, white teeth and cheerful faces, like a crowd at a festival. A few American soldiers in camouflage uniforms were talking by a jeep in the shadow of a tree, not even bothering to keep their rifles cocked. They were astonishingly tall. Manase did not know how he had ended up here, and felt misplaced. He remembered feeling ashamed of the rags hanging from his body—all that remained of his uniform.

Later, when he followed his memories, he seemed to recall that at daybreak he had crawled down to the river where they always got their water. The descent into the valley and the long climb back always exhausted his weak body, so his thirst must have been overwhelming. He remembered washing his hands because they were too dirty to scoop water. The grime looked like clotted blood, and no matter how he washed, the red cloud kept spreading in the water. He dipped his face into the stream and drank; then he must have fainted from exhaustion and been carried to the square. Manase did not know what happened to the soldiers in the cave. He recognized none of the other prisoners of war in the village square, and later in the camp he heard not a word about the cave. The lance corporal had been on the verge of death, but Manase thought how horrible it would have been if the intrepid captain also had rotted away from hunger and disease, cursing fate for denying his chance to cross swords with the enemy. But with the sudden twist in Manase's own fate, his recollections of the cave faded quickly.

The jungle shimmered in the heat; the undersides of the leaves were a blinding green. Manase remained seated on the baking sand, his head unprotected against the blazing sun, awaiting the vans that would take him and the other prisoners to the harbor of Ormoc. They must have looked miserable, for to the half-mocking, half-approving comments of his comrades, a gray-eyed American soldier walked past the rows of Japanese and drolly offered each soldier a cigarette, and as each defeated soldier bowed briefly to thank him, he lit it for him with a lighter the size of which none of them had seen before. Manase stared at the glowing tip of his cigarette seeming to vanish in the glaring sunlight, and sucked the smoke into his lungs. Only then did he realize he had been taken prisoner. He looked up. Over him burnt the sun, in a sky so blue that it almost seemed black.

The soldier beside him removed a brocade amulet from around his neck. I suppose he's grateful just to be alive, Manase thought, and now he wants to persuade himself it's true. But to his amazement the man walked up to the American who had given him the cigarette and gesticulated with hands and feet that he wanted to exchange the amulet for an entire pack. So that's how we'll have to live from now on, was the wordless message flashing through Manase's mind. Before finishing the thought he found himself checking for anything on him that he could barter.

Manase felt in the breast pocket of his jacket

and took out a little gray stone, finely marbled with green. He rolled it in the palm of his hand and decided with a sigh that it wouldn't bring a cent. Still he could not persuade himself to throw it away.

Manase had dedicated himself to his hobby for more than ten years, reaching the point at which his geological expertise—despite the autodidact's lopsidedness—matched that of any specialist in the field. Yet the bookseller in him realized that someone who has not undergone even the most elementary academic training can hardly present himself as a scholar. He therefore separated work and pleasure, never forgetting his real profession. Business was good—possibly because the bookstore was located near the center of the city; he expanded and renovated his shop and hired a few employees, though Manase refused to leave his work to others. Every morning he bicycled faithfully to his store where he spent the day helping customers, taking orders, arranging books. But the evenings were reserved for his hobby, from the moment he returned home till the moment he went to bed.

After dinner he would pick up the mug of tea his wife had poured for him and take it to his attic. There he smoked a cigarette and sipped his hot tea, letting his eyes wander over the racks of specimens. Then he resumed his work where he had ended the night before. He switched on a lamp on his desk and began polishing a section on a glass plate. Every now and then he would hold it up against the light to check for irregularities. He polished, bit by minuscule bit, with all the care his fingertips allowed. At the slightest suspicion of roughness indicating the presence of a coarser particle in the stone, he would rinse the glass plate in a tub of water, carefully removing all the dirt with an old toothbrush, and continue polishing with another abrasive. It was exhausting work, but because he was consumed by his task, two or three hours passed in what seemed a second. One section might take from three days to a week, depending on the material, so if after all that effort the specimen came out nicely, his emotion was all the stronger for it. Once the stone's surface had acquired a satisfactory gloss, he glued the section under a cover glass, scraped off the excess Canada balsam with a pocketknife, stuck on a label with the name and site of origin, and the job was done. After placing the finished section under the microscope, he would fill a wineglass with the grape juice his father-in-law sent him each year (since he did not drink alcohol) and raise a solitary toast. Then, calmly, he switched on the microscope lamp, trying to control the beating of his heart as he brought his eye to the lens. Of course he also owned a commercial set of sections, neatly arranged in a box, but even if the stone he was about to observe might have slight flaws, he had dug it up himself and processed it entirely with his own hands, and to the eye that peered through the lens, that knowledge made all the difference.

Each rock-forming mineral has its own chemical composition and its own characteristic refractive index. Under the white light of a polarizing microscope, they display interference colors resembling those of the rainbow, in combinations so bold and variegated that they stunned him each time with the miracle of their beauty. A scarlet shaft flashing through a field of cool blue; red, green, and yellow cheerfully intermingling as on a ship in full bunting; pale turquoise enveloped in a solid ring of black-speckled gray. The fabric woven by crystals and groundmass is a breathtakingly delicate natural design. The icicles in plagioclase hang so close together that they block your field of vision; the light and dark tiles of calcite form an intricate mosaic; the snowfield of quartz extends as far as the eye can reach; rectangular spaceships of mica and feldspar fly through a black night sky past an enormous yellow hornblende moon.

At such moments Manase always recalled the lance corporal's words in the Leyte cave. *A stone is the condensed history of the earth.* The phrase would tremble in his mind, and because he increasingly shared the same opinion, he would nod and cast another glance through the lens. The crystals lay still and motionless, hemmed in between two plates of glass, but eventually, after an endless period of time by human standards, these crystals might begin to grow again. Under heat and pressure their nondescript, expressionless, noncrystalline groundmass might even produce new crystals or perhaps break up and melt. For this solitary second the eternal cycle of matter, with its everlasting changes, had been frozen.

If he stared long enough at the mineral tapestries flickering under the microscope, the crystals seemed to possess an inner urge to grow. This urge had been forcibly repressed by some sort of magic keeping them locked inside this narrow space, but if that spell was somehow broken, would not the minerals burst into movement? Would not the crystals begin to move before his eyes—clash, intermingle, or perhaps collapse in demonstration of the infinite process of transformation? All at once the world under his eyes appeared to come to life, each mineral seemed a living creature, the crystals squirming. Through the narrow window of his microscope lens he saw the entire history of the earth. He witnessed the cosmos. He was no longer able to look away from the lens, and in his rapture he followed the dizzying creation and ruin of the crystals. His heart throbbed at the thought that he had glimpsed a universe whose true shape seldom revealed itself.

When at last the pain in his eyes became too much and he raised them from the microscope, his familiar storehouse attic would reappear before him, but its walls, desks, ceiling, the entire room seemed wondrously strange—solid, yet decidedly uncrystalline. At one moment he thought he saw a world in which everything had assumed the form of crystals, and now it seemed to him as if that world were swiftly fading, withdrawing. At once fearful and ecstatic, Manase surrendered once more to the magic and fixed his eyes upon the lens again.

When he heard the crowing of the neighbor's rooster Manase realized it was almost dawn. He put away his tools, glanced with his bloodshot eyes at his study, climbed down the steep ladder, and returned to the main house.

CHAPTER TWO

EVEN AS A LITTLE CHILD, Manase's son Hiroaki showed an interest in stones. At the slightest opportunity he would follow his father up the ladder to the storehouse attic, where he would gape at the specimens on the racks and the instruments on the desk and watch with fascination as his father worked. Manase had stored sulfuric acid, hydrogen peroxide, and poisons in his room, and because he was afraid his son might sneak in alone, he locked the storehouse and hid the key. But he enjoyed the visits from the young scientist.

Manase had not intended to teach his son about stones, but no sooner had the boy learned to talk than he began pointing at the racks and asking questions. Manase patiently named each stone and let him dust off the specimens and, occasionally, even look through the microscope. Oh, well, Manase thought, as soon as he finds a friend to play with he won't come up to this gloomy attic. But Hiroaki never tired of it. At least once a day his little head would peek out from the stairwell, and he was never without the geological picture book his father had bought for him, even in his sleep. Manase was biased, of course, but there was no denying that Hiroaki possessed a very good memory. Terms such as hornblende-gabbro or olivine basalt—expressions that gave the average amateur trouble—he rattled off in a way that amazed the adults. Before long he was bringing stones into the house and holding them up for his father's inspection while he proudly demonstrated how well he could classify them: "This one is granite. This one is limestone."

At first Manase was unsure whether to feel happy about this. His somber reaction had been: he's my child, so he'll never amount to much. It'll only be a burden to the boy and ourselves if we expect too much of him. But after Hiroaki went to elementary school his progress was so swift that Manase began, very cautiously, to dream that his son would become a scientist. Manase subscribed to a scientific children's journal in Hiroaki's name, and on birthdays and other suitable occasions gave him presents such as a small microscope or a telescope for gazing at the stars. Hiroaki's mother frowned on this, fearing that the boy might become eccentric like his father; alternately, she appreciated Hiroaki's good mind. "Someday you'll go to college and become a scientist," she always told him, working even harder than her husband to plant into her son's small body the seed of a dream.

The summer Hiroaki turned ten, his father took him on his first field trip. They rose before dawn and got on their bicycles before six, knowing the trouble it would cause if Hiroaki's little brother Takaaki caught on. First they rode along the Arakawa River from Kuroya to Minano, stopping here and there to look at an interesting outcrop, and next they followed the Akabira upstream to the little town of Yoshida, where they wandered along the Aguma and Yoshida (tributaries of the Akabira) past old quarries and yet more outcrops.

Several years before, Manase had drawn a detailed route map of the area, and even with his eyes closed he could describe in detail what stratum or fault ran where; if asked to explain the area's soil conditions he could go on forever. He was careful not to do so with Hiroaki, however. Forcing all that knowledge on a fifth grader would discourage him, Manase thought, so he limited himself to elementary explanations about how to look at strata and the most important hammer-and-chisel techniques. Otherwise he let the boy do as he pleased. After all, Manase had started his hobby not out of scientific curiosity but for the simple pleasure of collecting and playing with unusual stones. He felt a natural happiness when he wandered through fields and hillsides, and the secret purpose of this trip was to share that happiness with his son.

On the other hand Manase assumed his son would not become a stonemason, so what use was it if he taught him the best way to split a rock? The real goal was to discover the pleasure of investigating stones and strata—in other words, the fascination not of technique but of knowledge. Manase wanted to open Hiroaki's eyes to the true appeal of science, and though he sometimes laughed at himself, the amateur, pontificating in this vein, his ambition remained undiminished.

To teach is to learn, the saying goes. So

then what is it that makes science fascinating? Manase wondered. He leafed through scholarly works, to see if he could squeeze wisdom from their pages, but finally he always returned to what the lance corporal had told him in the cave.

Even the plainest, most ordinary pebble has the history of the universe written on it.

From this point of view, a diamond costing millions and an ordinary pebble from a riverbed have the same worth. Manase discovered value and meaning that transcend the normal standards of this world; he rejoiced in being far above, looking over it all, and most important he understood that the world is created as it is and not otherwise—that is the spell cast by geology and science. This, in a nutshell, is how Manase understood the lance corporal's words, and this is how he felt that afternoon in the river valley as they sat under a tree and ate their lunch while Manase tried to explain to Hiroaki, perched next to him on a boulder, why geology was so interesting.

To start out of the blue with such abstract ideas would make no sense, and besides, Manase didn't feel comfortable using grand language, so he chose words a child could readily understand.

But to his embarrassment (and amusement too), he suddenly heard himself speaking in the voice of the lance corporal. Maybe he had imagined that voice as he lay shivering with malaria—maybe the man had never opened his mouth. Didn't it make more sense that Manase's words would belong to no one but himself—the natural result of the stubborn enthusiasm with which he, in his own amateurish fashion, had practiced geology all these years, and the wealth of experience he had gained in the process?

A bead of sweat hung from Hiroaki's nose. His bare neck and arms sticking out of his white undershirt also glistened with sweat. Cheap celluloid toy sunglasses he had bought at a fair booth for use as eye guards were strapped over his forehead. With his white baseball cap and purple glasses Hiroaki looked like some cartoon hero on television, running from rock to rock tapping on stones, holding a hammer in gloves several sizes too big for him. Manase could not remember how many times he had smiled at the sight of his son that morning. Now Hiroaki's big eyes, inherited from his mother, were fixed on Manase as he listened silently while his father talked. The summer sun, no longer so hot, fell softly through the leaves of the tree under which they sat and cast dappled patterns on the boulders by the riverside. Here and there the smooth water threw up a shower of white spray and echoed in their ears. The stones on the riverbed were bathed in brilliant colors. The stream that flowed through this valley lent the minerals a natural luster. It was an ideal spot to see rocks at their most beautiful.

After eating their meal of rice balls stuffed with pickled plums, they washed the green apples they had picked that morning. The apples were twisted and colorless and wormy, but still the fresh juice did not taste bad.

After lunch there was a quiz: Manase picked a stone for Hiroaki to identify. Whenever they went for a walk to the Arakawa at dusk, Hiroaki pestered his father until he agreed to play. The first three questions Hiroaki answered easily, but then Manase handed him a gray stone.

"This one's difficult," said the boy as he caressed the stone to make certain of its touch. Manase loved to see Hiroaki like this, holding the stone before him in both hands, his head bowed slightly, as if making a ceremonial offering. He reminded his father of someone lost in prayer, and although Manase did not believe in anything, a moment like this reminded him how small human beings really are in the scheme of things, and his heart trembled with mysterious emotion.

Hiroaki cut a cross-section and studied it under his loupe but he wasn't satisfied, so he took out his tester kit—a beautiful wooden box his father had given him before the summer vacation, with ten mineral samples arranged in ascending order of hardness. It was not practical in the field, but it had been unthinkable for Hiroaki to go on his first expedition without this instrument, so brand-new that the box still smelled of varnish. The budding mineralogist started with talc, Mohs' hardness 1, and continued up the scale with gypsum, calcite, and fluorite—taking each one out of the box to scratch the stone with. Manase wanted to tell him that he would get faster results if he used a needle or a pin. You can teach too much too fast, he thought; better to let Hiroaki first try things by himself, so he said nothing and looked on with a smile. Finally Hiroaki seemed to realize he had failed, for he blushed and fluttered his eyelashes, but then he looked up suddenly and said: "Diabase!"

Manase had given his son a challenging stone, and in his amazement nearly asked how he had chosen the correct answer, but one look at his son's face revealed that the stone's light-green tinge provided the clue. Actually, with diabase, color is generally not a reliable indicator, but still, Manase gave his son an encouraging pat on the back. Diabase has very small crystals, he explained, so it is difficult to distinguish this kind of stone from dolerite or diorite without preparing a section and observing the orientation of the pyroxene and plagioclase crystals under a microscope; and that was exactly what he proposed doing as soon as they got home.

"And will you let me do it?" asked Hiroaki. He looked at his father with eyes screwed into narrow slits, as if the sun was too bright for them. He already knew the answer would be yes.

Out of a perverse desire to tease him, Manase allowed a doubtful note to creep into his voice: "I guess so. Are you sure you can do the whole thing yourself?"

"Of course I can! I'll do the grinding slowly and carefully. I'll need your help only at the end when I glue it on the glass."

This is the way the son leaves the father behind, thought Manase. In time, Hiroaki will grow up, and probably never think back on the father who gave him his first geology lessons. He nodded wistfully, and Hiroaki lowered his head as if he knew and grieved for what his father felt in his heart. After a brief silence, in which he appeared to listen to the stream rippling in the gorge, Hiroaki put the specimen into his backpack.

After lunch they bicycled farther upstream along the Akabira River to an old quarry near the hamlet of Matsuida. Here the hills had been so deeply excavated that they formed a high cliff in which the strata were clearly visible, from the Paleozoic Chichibu stratum with chert and slate at the bottom to a Quaternary layer of gravel on top—a true treasure house of fossils. Seen from the sun-baked rock floor at the foot of the cliff, the lush green of the surrounding forest stood in dazzling contrast to the white limestone below.

Hiroaki stared silently at the outcrops in the cliffs. He had learned a simple way to distinguish fossils and collect specimens, but he seemed dissatisfied with the results and soon began running from one spot to another. Suddenly he cried out. Behind the tall tufts of grass at the far end of the cliff he had found a gaping black hole. Even Manase, who had been here often, had never noticed the existence of a cave, and when he looked more closely, he decided it was probably an old trial shaft made by miners prospecting for limestone.

Hiroaki parted the dense curtain of creepers and thorny briers and stooped to look inside the cave. He was hit by a cold, dank smell. Manase laughed at his son's fear. It was all very well to be cautious, but a boy had to have some guts. Manase was already satisfied there was no danger, but he was tempted by the spirit of adventure and creeped into the hole first.

The interior of the cave was barely high enough for an adult to walk hunched over. The shaft was about ten feet wide, and in places the walls had been shored up with planks to prevent cave-ins. After only fifteen feet or so their way was barred by a wooden partition. Although it had not been their intention to go very far, so deep below the surface, this was such an abrupt end to their exploration that it hardly deserved the name of adventure. Manase lit a match to inspect the walls and noticed they partly consisted of a remarkably fine stratum of green chert, but the rest was nothing special.

"Green chert. What kind of stone is that?" asked Hiroaki, his voice reverberating in the chilly air of the cave.

"A sedimentary rock formed by the skeletons of Paleozoic organisms."

Organisms like conodonts and radiolarians, explained Manase; the green color was from iron oxide.

"Do you think there's a Paleoparadoxia here?" Hiroaki asked, hoarse with excitement, as he patted the walls with his hand.

"Who knows?"

"And fossils of Mesozoic dinosaurs?"

"I don't think so. But it sure looks as if you'd be able to find some pretty good fossils here."

Manase was lying, but Hiroaki had addressed him as a friend with whom he was sharing a secret, and that made Manase so happy he found it impossible to answer any other way. To add extra color to this small father-and-son adventure, he promised that they would return with a better lamp and continue their exploration.

After using up the matches, Manase followed Hiroaki to the entrance. Outside, the late-afternoon heat and the strong fragrance of grass enveloped his body. His eyes had grown accustomed to the dark, and he closed them tight against the glare of the sun. When he slowly opened them again, the green of the forest was like a burning black flame. It was time they went home, Manase said, but Hiroaki laughed, having shed his fear of only a few minutes before. He looked at the sun high in the sky, and with a heroic gesture put on his toy glasses. "Just a little bit longer!" he cried and dashed over to an outcrop, which he assaulted with his hammer—the cartoon hero in shorts and shirtsleeves. Manase smiled and observed the budding geologist, oblivious to the sun burning his skin in the shadeless quarry.

Back from the field trip, Hiroaki announced he had decided on a suitable physics project for his summer vacation assignment: he would put together a collection of stone specimens. Evening after evening he eagerly climbed to the storehouse attic and worked at the desk his father had built for him, the smell of mosquito incense wafting about him. The entire summer Manase had Hiroaki beside him. "Oh, I wish the summer would never end," the son sighed one day, choked with emotion, but perhaps it was the father who should have made that wish.

All Manase could remember of that summer was the light pouring over everything. Time and again, trying to recall all that had happened, he looked back on those days, always feeling as if he were trying to chase an ebbing dream. Maybe it had all been impossible from the start, he and Hiroaki, floating in a transparent vessel filled with light. The vessel drifted before his eyes, but when he reached out it moved away, and if he suddenly grabbed for it the vision burst like a soap bubble. Was the past nothing more than a momentary illusion, unrelated to his real self?

Fifth graders are simply not interested in geology. Boys that age only want to play—the muddier the better. Hiroaki was no weakling, nor was he any clumsier than anyone else, yet he never hung around the neighborhood kids; instead he hunted for stones in the river or read illustrated geology books. Manase had sometimes worried about this and often encouraged Hiroaki to play with his friends, but he was optimistic enough to believe that sooner or later Hiroaki would acquire the necessary social skills. He seemed confident and chose his words with precocious care, even when talking to his father—but wasn't that a deviation from the norm? That summer Hiroaki had taken in a great deal of knowledge very fast, partly because he had a dedicated, patient teacher by his side, but mostly because of his own enthusiasm. It wasn't as if Hiroaki acted old for his age, but it was increasingly obvious that he was different. Had his existence been an illusion, or perhaps the crystallization of a dream bestowed on Manase as a gift?

At night, alone in the storehouse, Manase would stare at the clumsily arranged stones in the cookie box, each labeled in childish, penciled characters, and his memory's floodgates would burst, drowning everything in sight. And finally the swirling stream of Manase's visions would reach that one spot of calm water where he lay floundering, struggling against the inevitable, and sweep over him. Dreams always fade. The more precious the gift, the higher its price.

Hiroaki died that summer toward the end of August, a few days before the end of his vacation. Early in the afternoon he had gone for a ride on his bicycle, but when he did not return after dark, his worried mother and the neighbors organized search parties. The next morning someone noticed a child's bicycle in a quarry near Matsuida, and a policeman discovered

Hiroaki's body in a tunnel in a cliffside. Hiroaki's Mohs' hardness tester had been found in the basket of his bicycle; his hammer, clinometer, and magnifying glass lay next to his body—all things Manase had given him.

Manase was not home: he had been on a night train heading west to a reunion of the Kyoto Society of Amateur Geologists. On his arrival at his hotel he was handed a telegram, and he returned without delay. He was back in Chichibu the same evening. There he found Hiroaki's body in the funeral chapel of the hospital, shrouded in white linen, watched by his wife. Her face was expressionless, empty. Her tears had dried long before.

The official cause of death was excessive loss of blood due to stab wounds. Hiroaki's face and upper body had been mutilated by cuts and slashes inflicted with a sharp weapon. There had been a series of similar cases, in which the victims had invariably been boys, from northwestern Saitama to the bordering prefecture of Gunma, so the police assumed this was the work of the same person. As soon as news arrived that a suspicious man had been seen near the quarry on the afternoon of the crime, a sketch of the suspect was posted on street corners. Days and months passed without a clue. The investigation reached a dead end.

Manase had never been sociable, and after the incident he increasingly withdrew into his attic—but no longer to occupy himself with his stones; he did not even feel like looking at them. The original reason he hid in the storehouse and bolted its door upon arriving at home in the evening was to escape his wife's persecution. "It's your fault Hiroaki is dead!" she reproached him every day.

Bereft of words, Manase exposed himself to his wife's attacks. First came the endless complaints and accusations; those were not so bad so long as Manase bore them silently until she had drunk herself into a stupor, but soon she found his very meekness unbearable. Am I talking to a wall?" she screamed, stretching out her hand to his cheek as if to make certain he was a human being standing before her. And then she attacked him in a blind rage, without caring where she hit him.

Manase understood very well his wife's hysteria. But despite his willingness to swallow the violent accusations and take care of her until her wound healed, even he could not bear her physical attacks. When he defended himself she became furious and began yelling insults that carried throughout the neighborhood. Finally she lost all control and began hurling ashtrays and glasses at his head; Manase sought refuge in the storehouse.

His wife had always drunk. She would stand in the kitchen and, with a contemptuous glance at her husband, pour a bit into a teacup. But after Hiroaki's death she switched from sake to whisky, and she was drunk every day by one or two in the afternoon. She let her household deteriorate. Takaaki, their younger son, regularly threw tantrums over the most trivial things and lay screaming. He also began to wet his bed, something he had never done. Almost every morning his bedclothes were wet, and his mother would give him a ferocious beating. But she hardly gave him anything to eat; many evenings the neighbors would see him in the garden chewing on a cucumber until they could no longer stand the sight and occasionally fed him. Finally Manase's elder sister in Chichibu more or less adopted him.

Forty-nine days after Hiroaki's death—the end of the mourning period—Manase discovered his wife in the darkness of the storehouse. After the last memorial service had ended and the priest had gone home, Manase went to his bookstore; when he returned home that evening and climbed up the ladder to the attic, he found his wife sitting alone in the darkness. Her being in the storehouse wasn't suspicious, for he had given her a key to the door, but he was startled all the same. He was about to ask what she was doing there, but swallowed the words just in time and turned on the light.

Manase's wife had seldom visited his study during their marriage; the last time had been shortly after their wedding. This had never seemed strange to Manase, but now he realized she had always done her best to respect her husband's privacy. She was sitting at Hiroaki's desk and one by one took the displayed possessions of her dead son into her hands. Manase feared this would cause a new attack of grief, nor could he suppress a growing sense that she was intruding.

"Is there perhaps a reason you don't want me here?"

Although the mornings and evenings were already chilly, she wore a thin, sleeveless dress, exposing her naked bony shoulders. Her dark skin, on which swollen veins were visible, was covered with dirt. Around her left eye was a black bruise. He did not know how she had got it.

"What did you do here all the time? And always in secret?"

She did not seem drunk. Though lately she had been inseparable from the bottle, she appeared to have left it at home this time. Manase could see that any answer he gave might provoke a new outburst of resentment, so he said nothing and sat down silently on the chair next to her.

"You were doing something terrible here, that much I knew. I knew, but I didn't let on— I was too scared to say anything. I was so frightened when Hiro started coming here; you have no idea. And the child was frightened too, you know. Frightened to come here. He didn't really want to."

Any words of consolation, he knew, would sound hollow. Time passed in silence, second by second. She was trembling—whether with cold or with anger he did not know. She had been twenty when they married, a young girl with the face of a child who had thickened within a single year. Yet, as he saw her now, shivering and with purple lips, he saw again her slender back arched over the family's vegetable plots just after she had come to live with him, a sullen look on her face because there was nothing else for her to do as long as her mother-in-law was strong enough to run the household.

"What did you teach him here? What did you have in mind?"

The father had lured the son to his death— that delusion had taken hold of her after the endless torment of her loss, and every time Manase heard it he felt a sandstorm of grief swirl around his heart. But if it would satisfy her, if it helped her escape the void, he was prepared to confess that he had murdered Hiroaki.

"What did you do to the child?"

A deep gloom settled over Manase. The endless interrogation was beginning, again, and he was preparing for the worst when he realized his wife was no longer cursing him; all he felt was her anguish. Could it be that she was edging, ever so slightly, away from the abyss? Manase felt as if he had discovered an infinitesimal point of light at the bottom of a muddy bog. He looked at the person sitting before him. Silently, one by one, his wife picked up the specimens on the desk. Perhaps this was the right moment to speak to her tenderly, to restore their relationship, to escape from their ruined marriage as husband and wife. Manase studied her pale profile and searched for words. Was there a relationship to be restored? And supposing they did escape—where could they go? The tendrils of his heart, stretching toward the light, withered again. He was trying to restore the utterly and undeniably empty shell of their relationship. Before marriage he had lived in his attic like a barnacle. Had he ever made an attempt to leave? And what was he? The owner of a gloomy storehouse who showed his face in the main house to play father and husband. That was all.

From the deep shadows cast by the naked light bulb on the specimen racks, rows of stones stared down at the silent couple. A cricket chirped, though where it was was unclear.

"Oh, well, what's done is done, and what can you do about it," said his wife.

What's done is done. Since the funeral Manase had heard that phrase a thousand times.

"At least I still have Takaaki. Do you know, I love him a lot more than I did Hiro?"

That, too, was not news to Manase, but she seemed to pay remarkably little attention to Takaaki. Her insistence that she had hung all her hopes on her remaining son only showed how difficult it was for the one to fill the gap left by the other. The dry tone in which his wife mentioned Takaaki contrasted so sharply with the content of her words that it left Manase impassive.

"Stay away from Takaaki. I beg you, don't take that child away from me too," his wife said.

She turned her face toward her husband. Her cheeks were hollow, her eyes bloodshot. Manase looked away.

"Promise me. Please. Promise me you will stay away from the child."

If he were to casually say the words she demanded from him, he knew it would provoke an explosion; yet, cornered by those glaring eyes, he could not resist. "All right, I promise." Her hair standing on end, her eyes burning with anger, she threw the stone straight between his eyes, laying open his forehead. Manase saw it happening. Then she bowed her head and became silent again.

His feet were getting cold. There was not even enough oil in the stove to warm himself. He switched on the hot plate to make tea, but when he saw that the kettle was empty, he switched it off.

His wife was weeping. Her sobs echoed against the high stone walls of the storehouse, her tears fell on the desk.

"Oh, but I know," she said, her voice trembling. "Someday, Takaaki will die too. I know very well. It'll be just the same with him as with Hiro."

Forsaken and abandoned. The words would not come. He had to do something, and he started to get up from his chair. Half standing, he looked at his wife. She held another stone in her hand. That's biotite granite, he almost blurted out, but stopped. A woman is inconsolable with grief, and the man before her is showing off his knowledge about stones. For a moment this abominable scenario was all he could see, and his taut face slowly bent into a grin.

He sank into his chair. He felt only emptiness inside. His ears registered a long series of weak sobs—not pleas for sympathy or pity but the unmistakable voice of loneliness itself. From a distance Manase observed his heart weeping.

Finally his wife got up, walked silently to the ladder as if unaware of her husband's presence, and disappeared into the dark. Manase sat in his chair and listened, until the storehouse door closed behind her with a soft click.

In Manase's absence, his wife had had to identify their son's body. The image of his cruelly mistreated face was branded into her eyes. She no longer bathed or slept on a mattress, she no longer even ate, and all day long she lay on the bare planks of the kitchen floor reeking of whisky. If Takaaki disappeared for even a moment, she would run through the neighborhood raving that "that man" was now trying to kill her remaining son. When astonished neighbors listened to her story in an attempt to calm her down, they learned that "that man" was her own husband. Everyone felt sorry for her, but her derangement became so extreme that she began to frighten people.

It was a hopeless case, it would end badly—everyone saw the approaching catastrophe, but no one lifted a finger. Her husband received all the blame, for it seemed he was only avoiding the problem. Yet Manase was no passive onlooker. He had consulted the social workers assigned to the neighborhood, and they said her alcoholism needed immediate treatment. But how was he going to persuade her to check into a hospital? She pounced on him at every chance, eager to dig her fingernails deep into his face. One day, at wit's end, Manase took a length of rope from the storehouse.

I'm taking her to a hospital today, come what may; when she's too tired to stay awake tonight, I'll tie her up, and then I'll drag her along if necessary. His plans were hopelessly confused. He might succeed in tying her up, but how was he going to take her into town—carry her over his shoulders? Besides, most hospitals are closed at night.

Manase managed to slip into the house according to plan, rope in hand. When he peeked through the kitchen door he saw, by the light of the gibbous moon, a black shadow on the wooden floor: his wife was asleep, snoring. In three strides he was at her side, but when he touched her oddly hot body she sat up. He refused to let this affect him, and pushed her to the floor. When she started screaming that she was being killed, he began believing that he really had brought the rope to strangle her. Both of them dead—what a relief. He looped a noose around her neck and tightened it. Then something hit him on the head, stunning him.

There stood his wife, her hair disheveled, a baleful fire burning in her eyes, a whisky bottle in her right hand. She threw the bottle aside, grabbed a kitchen knife from the sink, and lunged. The knife glittered pale in the moonlight, but what truly horrified him was the bloodlust to which he had almost given in. He ran through the tall weeds in the yard to the storehouse, and locked the door. Still gasping for breath, he heard his wife outside screaming: "Murderer! Murderer!"

The neighbors must have thought that something really terrible indeed had happened this time, or perhaps the piercing screams were finally more than their nerves could bear, for somebody called the police. Within minutes a car arrived with a few officers, who wrested the knife away from the distraught woman.

As everyone more or less expected, Manase's wife was forced to enter a hospital. Three months later her alcoholism was under control and she was allowed to go home, but instead of returning to her husband and son she went to her parents' house to recuperate. After about two months Manase was visited by a social worker who had been asked by his father-in-law to see if he would agree to a divorce.

Manase visited his wife only once at her parents' home in Yamanashi. He was shown into a large, sunny room with a view of a garden with chickens and a surprisingly tall Mount Fuji. He waited until she entered. Her color was healthy, and she appeared to have gained some weight. For a moment Manase hoped they might yet be reunited as a family. Then she saw him, and her face changed into a Nōh mask with malevolent eyes. "You're the one who killed Hiroaki! You killed him in that cave!" Manase heard the dark menace in her voice and knew it was over. Seen out of the door by her grave-looking relatives, he returned home.

Manase's wife had surrendered custody of Takaaki, and Manase was eager to care for the boy, but it is very hard for a single man to raise a child alone. More important, Takaaki appeared to dislike his father: when he saw his face, his mouth began to work and he started crying. Manase saw little choice but to offer his sister a generous monthly stipend for Takaaki's lodging and care. His brother-in-law, who owned a fertilizer company in Chichibu, was an easygoing man with many children by his wife and other women. He hardly noticed the presence of one more in his house, and Manase's sister was very fond of her only nephew. She thought—and everyone agreed—that the boy would be better off with his roughhousing cousins than alone with his melancholy father.

For a while the murder was daily front-page news, but the rumors that had made parents shiver died down. The dark shadow of the bestial crime skimmed away over their heads, swift as a bird in flight. The sketches of the suspect rotted on their telephone poles under rain and wind and were now nowhere to be seen.

Manase could not bear the loneliness of the deserted house and soon returned to his storehouse attic. For days he stared at Hiroaki's old desk, imagining he could still see the shade of his dead child; endlessly he fondled the few little things his son had left behind. Then he had an idea: he would complete Hiroaki's unfinished collection and place it as an offering on his grave. For the first time in months he roamed past outcrops with his hammer and mixed chemicals in water to wash his specimens.

The cookie box with the clumsily arranged stones contained thirty cardboard sections, and three of them were still empty. Manase tried to imagine what Hiroaki would have wanted to fill them with. Green chert—he had no idea about the other two stones, but he was certain about green chert. When Hiroaki went to the Matsuida quarry that day he must have remembered his father telling him about a stratum of green chert in the walls of the cave. Manase found a specimen, though not in the same spot, and cleaned it. When he placed it into the box he cried harder than he had during Hiroaki's funeral.

After finishing his son's memorial collection Manase again began to busy himself with stones. He was overwhelmed with requests for classifications or polished sections. For a long time he had simply put them aside, but now he answered the letters in the order in which they had arrived. It occurred to him that he ought to donate sets of specimens to elementary and junior high schools in the area. For a while this occupied him. As for his work at the bookstore, his employees realized Manase could not concentrate on the business, and made sure it did not suffer. In fact, the ripples of the economic boom had finally reached these distant shores, and sales were actually increasing. In this respect, at least, Manase had reason to be content.

Every morning he went to the neighborhood

store to buy a roll and milk for breakfast; after working in the bookstore all day he ate a quick meal downtown, then went home to work in his attic deep into the night. His life resumed its steady rhythm. When the weather was fine you could see him getting off his bicycle at the foot of the bridge, smoking a cigarette and looking out over the Chichibu Mountains.

Knowing that a single man leads an inconvenient life (and possibly also because they suspected he had put aside a tidy sum), charitable persons would from time to time offer to help the melancholy middle-aged man find a bride. But once they saw his pale, expressionless face peeking through the storehouse window, most turned around and left without saying a word. Manase did not feel like remarrying, and from the moment he had started living on his own again he believed that a sad, lonely place suited his character best. He found it almost impossible to imagine that he had once had a family—it seemed unreal, something from a distant past. Events from the war, on the other hand, he remembered with increasing clarity: *this* had happened in *this* month of *that* year, and *that* event on *this* day at *that* time. Before long he was pinning dates on more or less everything, and soon he began hearing the voice of the lance corporal in the cave on Leyte. He realized this was not normal, but since it did not interfere with his daily life he refused to let it bother him. The voice summoned long-lost memories. When he heard the lance corporal trying to persuade him that geology was really very interesting, for instance, he would break into a big smile. Manase also began to talk when he was alone—not to the lance corporal, but to the shade of Hiroaki. Whenever he was working in his attic it was as if he saw his son sitting across from him, and he would carefully explain the significance of each stage of the project at hand, as if teaching him. Still, because he remained alert to what others would think if they heard him going on like this, he managed to keep somewhat involved in society. If Manase's psychological condition was at all abnormal, its prime cause had to be sought in his dreams, for Manase suffered increasingly from nightmares.

He had not been near the Matsuida quarry since that fateful day, but late in the fall, while gathering fossils along the upper reaches of the Akabira, he became so engrossed in his work that he forgot himself until it began to grow dark. Hastily he pedaled home, and as he watched the blazing colors in the river valley melt into darkness, he discovered he was riding down the forest road that led to the quarry. It was the shortest way from the Akabira valley back to his house and in the past he had used it often. But the fossil bivalve he had discovered at the end of the day appeared to belong to a species he had never seen before, and his impatience to look more closely had made him careless. The road curved away from the river and up into the hills, the asphalt turned to a rough gravel surface. Then he saw the cliff of the quarry to his left. For a second he wondered if he should not simply continue, but on reaching the naked limestone open space he stopped. He would have to visit the spot at least once, he'd often told himself, and that he had unwittingly come this way after having avoided the place for so long suggested the impact of the shock had abated sufficiently for him to make a reckoning. This might be his chance. Perhaps his heart had been secretly yearning for just such an opportunity. With long strides Manase walked toward the cliff. There was the cave. The weeds around it had been mown short, and the entrance had been boarded up. The door had been securely fastened with barbed wire—not, it seemed to him, to prevent children from getting lost there again, but to seal off the fear caused by the terrible events inside. Manase winced as he imagined the tender skin of a child being torn by the sharp barbs.

He peered through a slit between the planks. All he could see was jet-black darkness. For a moment he thought he saw a wavering of light. Impossible, it can't be, he said to himself and rubbed his eyes. No, he was not mistaken, there was something shining faintly deeper inside. Outside it was dark, the mountains were deserted, and it would have been natural for him to run away, but instead of fear he felt only curiosity. He pushed his face against the planks to get a better view. Could it be ... was his son still alive? Perhaps he'd managed to escape and had been there in that dark spot all along, waiting for help. Though it was an absurd notion, Manase knew suddenly that it had to be true. He was consumed with impatience. He grabbed his hammer and chisel, cut the barbed wire with a few sharp, well-aimed blows, and lifted the door off its hinges.

Half crouching, he entered the cave. He could still see the light. Almost immediately he was at the wooden partition. Where had the light gone? It came from the other side. Although the planks had been firmly nailed against a wooden frame, in the darkness they had rotted, and he did not even have to use a tool to pry them loose. He easily made an opening big enough to crawl through. When he stood up on the other side, the ceiling of the cave was higher than his head. He could feel a current of wet, warm air. Manase took a few more steps and found the source of the strange light. It was a campfire.

On a rock sat a man dressed in a straw-colored uniform, a red-striped army cap on his head, one of his legs wrapped tightly in puttees. The flames flickered red over one half of his body, and behind him a massive black shadow writhed that seemed to have an intelligence all its own. Every now and then a branch exploded in the fire, but the rest of the cave was shrouded in a deadly hush. If he listened carefully, he could hear someone groaning and muttering softly in the darkness.

The man at the fire held a sword in his hand. As he pulled it from the scabbard, Manase began to tremble. The flash of the blade in the darkness dazzled him. The giant shadow on the wall bent forward and threw itself his way. Manase knew: he was *there*. But even as a scream of despair forced itself through his throat and distorted his lips, the sharp voice rang in his ears. "Manase!" The scream frozen in his mouth, the soldier in him jumped to attention and barked the answer: "Here!"

"Damn this bloody noise. It's keeping everyone awake! Manase, go kill him!"

The captain's lustrous voice grabbed him by the guts and bones—the voice that broke over him like a dark wave and forced its way into the smallest cavities of his body. Not only was resistance unthinkable, but the horror of the captain's order had vanished. He knew whom he had to kill; the voice that sounded from the depths of the cave was the lance corporal's, talking about stones. Manase walked past the fire to the wall near the entrance to the cave, where a man was lying on his back whispering. It was clear the man's life was burning out fast. All the more reason to spare him more suffering, Manase told himself as he reached for his bayonet. Then he noticed he was not carrying his rifle. His blood ran cold. A rifle is a soldier's life, and the consequences of losing it are dire. Sick with fear, the more he tried to remember where he had left it, the less he remembered. He was looking around when the voice arose behind him again.

"Get on with it, man! What are you waiting for?"

"Yes, sir!" he answered with all the energy he could muster. With eyes blinking desperately he tried to think how to make up for his blunder.

"Use this sword," called the captain from beside the fire. Manase had no time to understand the reason for this unexpected order, or to feel relief at having escaped his predicament. He ran straight to the captain and grabbed the sword with trembling hands.

"You'd like to try this out on a human being, wouldn't you?"

The captain appeared to be smiling, but the private was standing at attention—ramrod straight, eyes on the middle distance—he could not make out the face of his commanding officer.

"Oh, I know. I saw you looking at it," the captain said. "You ought to see your eyes!"

Now he was sure the captain was smiling. He heard it in his voice.

"Well, all right then, I'll let you use it. Cut to your heart's content. See if you develop the taste. Then you'll know more in one second than you've learned in your entire life."

The captain was no longer smiling, and his voice sounded much sterner while he instructed Manase how best to kill a human being with a sword. Careful not to cut yourself in the legs. Hold the hilt about as firmly as you'd hold a heavy umbrella. Above all, no slashing or thrusting. And you don't need to use a crazy amount of force; just rest the point on the skin and, in the time it takes to inhale, pull the sword very lightly around, as if cutting through water. He had Manase repeat these instructions, then nodded.

"All right then, Manase. Go ahead." His voice was soft but urgent.

Sword raised, Manase walked cautiously to the dying man and looked down at him again. All thought had disappeared. He had even forgotten who it was he was about to kill—all that remained were the words he had been made to repeat. After some hesitation he decided that the simplest way to go about it was to cut the carotid artery. He switched the sword to his left hand so he could pull open the man's uniform with his right until the grimy neck lay bare down to the chest. Then he took the hilt again in both hands. Slowly, as if feeling its own way, the tip of the sword searched for its target. As the captain's eyes burned his back, Manase muttered his instructions one more time, to be sure. All right then. Here we go, he thought. At that moment the lance corporal, who had been lying passively there, opened his eyes wide and stared Manase straight in the face.

"Wait until morning. I don't want to die until I've seen the sun rise one more time. Tomorrow morning I'll ask you to kill me. Let me live till then."

Orders are orders. Manase looked hesitantly at the fire, but the captain, his eyes fixed on the flames, told him to hurry. Then the man on the ground lifted a voice that vibrated with a life one would hardly expect in someone about to die; he hurled the words not at the trembling soldier with the sword, but at the officer who had given the order.

"Why are you killing me? Aren't wars fought so that men and nations may live? We die in order to live, we do not die for the sake of dying!"

"Kill him, Manase!"

The thunderous voice rends the air in the cave. A yellow light flashes behind Manase's eyes, all thought and feeling having left his head, only his muscles twitch spasmodically. He no longer gives a damn about the rules of swordsmanship, or any other rules. The man is about to say more, his mouth a gaping black hole. Manase brings the sword down with all the force he can muster. Numbness travels like lightning through his fingers, as if he has hit rock. He hears a scream. Oh, damn, I've hit him on the skull. I'm messing up again. Manase panics. He no longer knows what he is doing and slashes left and right—head, face, it doesn't matter where—to finish him off as soon as possible. But the more he panics, the more his frazzled nerves mechanically contract his muscles. He comes to and sees that the hands gripping the hilt are stained dark red. Still the man refuses to die. "Please! Please, don't!" The voice begging for mercy has suddenly changed into that of a child. . . .

Manase screams and opens his eyes. His mattress is soaked. He jumps up and runs to the sink. His throat is parched. He drinks from the faucet until he is about to burst, and only then does he realize it was a dream. He cannot stop trembling; he is still gripping the sword, and no matter how he washes and washes, the blood sticks to his hands.

Manase had more such dreams, and it was obvious to him that they were more than just nightmares. Memories are nothing but events that have changed into landscapes, and for people who have reached a certain age, the past holds more variety than the future, because they can paint the landscapes of their past. Manase's landscapes were worm-eaten. The canvases had black holes that became wider every day. They made it impossible for him to look back on his past in tranquillity; they slowly but surely gnawed away at his daily life.

Each nightmare showed in his face. His hair became grayer and his gums swelled so that he lost many teeth. Although Manase had only just entered middle age, every day he looked more like an old man.

CHAPTER THREE

TIME PASSED in its own way, indifferent to the activities of the hermit in the storehouse. Through the period of his family's disintegration, Manase's surviving son had shown no talent for anything but screaming, but under the watchful eye of his aunt, whose vigor seemed to increase with every child she had, he grew into a sturdy boy. Takaaki was good at soccer. Even before he entered elementary school he played soccer late into the evening—even on Sundays and holidays—and when he turned twelve he asked to be registered at a junior high school known for its soccer team. The school was in the city of Urawa, outside his own school district, and required a complicated commute of some fifteen miles each way, but Takaaki made the trip every day without complaint. By the following summer it was clear he would not be able to keep up this heavy schedule. Fortunately one of his older cousins went to college in Tokyo and lived in a boardinghouse in Nippori—at most half an hour by train from Urawa—so Takaaki moved into the same boardinghouse that fall.

Of course he joined the school soccer club, playing center back, the pivot of the entire team. What he lacked in agility and technique he more than made up for with superb speed and strong legs. He was proud of his ironclad defense, which could stop any ball in any scuffle, but at the slightest opportunity he would make furious sallies forward and use his height to intimidate the goalie. The main difference between Takaaki and his older brother was that Takaaki resembled his father more. As a child he had been just as short and slender, but once he reached puberty he shot up until his hairy thighs were as thick as a woman's waist and his muscles as hard as stone.

Because of his athletic prowess, Takaaki received scholarship offers from several high schools; he chose a private one in the Itabashi

Ward of Tokyo. He left his boardinghouse and moved in with the soccer coach, who also took in other players, all drawn from the remotest corners of the country for their extraordinary potential. Bunking with such comrades stimulated Takaaki's sense of rivalry, and he trained hard. At the beginning of his second year Takaaki became a starting player. The year before, his school had made it into the semifinals of the High School National Championship, and everyone dreamed of winning the cup. But their dream ended unexpectedly when the team was routed in the third round of the regional qualifications. In the swirling sand of the soccer field Takaaki and his teammates swore to avenge their loss, and for the next twelve months they trained twice as hard as the year before.

"The best training is an actual match!" their coach would shout, so every weekend they played two or three practice matches a day, not only against other high schools but also against university or company teams. By summer they had reached their goal of fifty matches, and over vacation they toured the country. By the new team's hundredth match it was fall, time for the regional qualifications.

The first game was against a public high

school from the Suginami Ward. Takaaki's team won 6–0. This was an auspicious start for their climb to the national championship, but not for Takaaki.

With only a few seconds left to play and the outcome virtually certain, Takaaki was tackled from behind. He retaliated by knocking down his opponent. If he had stopped there the whole affair might have blown over, but when the referee ran over to him to issue a warning Takaaki took a swing at him, a major offense. Of course there was a story connected to this. The referee was a university instructor critical of private schools that attracted top athletes. A few days before the tournament he had published an article in one of the daily papers headlined "No More Pros in School Sports," which clearly favored the Tokyo public schools. Takaaki was sent off the field. His left ankle appeared to be broken, so he was sent straight to the hospital. No sooner had he been discharged, leaning on crutches and his leg in a cast, than he heard he had been suspended for the rest of the tournament.

Manase had witnessed it all. After Takaaki went to live in Nippori, father and son rarely met. Between high school and college the relationship would have completely dissolved had it not been for the allowance Manase deposited in Takaaki's account each month. The first time Manase saw his grown son was when his sister took him to the soccer match in the autumn of Takaaki's third year at senior high. He sat in the corner bleachers, hardly recognizing the tall, strapping figure of Takaaki out on the field. It's amazing, he thought admiringly, how children grow up no matter what they go through. The sight of all those young men running in the cool breeze under the blue autumn sky lifted his spirits. He had been content to play the role of spectator, but now that Takaaki's team was clearly on its way to victory, he began to wonder if he should not say a few admiring or encouraging words to his son. Not that he assumed the relation between father and son could be restored immediately, or that Takaaki would agree to take care of him in his old age. But he hoped that Takaaki had grown up enough to forget his childhood grudge against his father. It would be enough if they could meet now and then, perhaps share a meal together. At the very least, he thought, this was an opportunity to tell Takaaki not to worry about money until he was ready to enter society as a responsible adult.

And Takaaki might not object to saying hello to the father who promised him financial support for the next few years.

Like a lean, alert, keen-nosed hound standing out in the middle of the pack, Takaaki dashed over the soccer field, and when Takaaki scored the sixth goal with a magnificent shot from midfield, his father jumped up from his seat, clapping and cheering. But Manase began to worry as the end of the match drew near. Would he get a chance to talk to Takaaki? The anxiety made him sick to his stomach, and it was then that Takaaki hit the referee in the face. Manase had not seen the punch clearly, but he could tell something had happened. All of a sudden the stadium froze, even the wind died down. In the deadly silence the sudden explosion of violence seemed more real.

Manase began to shiver. The moment he saw the lone player leave the field, dragging his injured left leg and refusing all offers of help from the bench, Manase knew his son had still not forgiven him. The number two on his jersey radiated a loneliness and hatred that seemed directed like a malevolent arrow straight at his father in the bleachers. Manase had the feeling that Takaaki had attacked the referee just to spite his father. Why did Takaaki hate him so much? he wondered. But in fact this was the first time he had ever tried to imagine what went on inside his son's mind. His elder son had been dead for years and yet he always thought of him, but most days he hardly remembered he had another child. Manase was appalled at himself. All that time he had never shown interest in Takaaki—the realization hit him like the lash of a whip. And now it was too late to recall that interest to life. Without a word, even to his sister, Manase left the stadium.

Takaaki's team lost in the finals of the regional qualifications, and their dream of the national championship evaporated. Before the tournament was over, Takaaki resigned from the club. His coach did not understand, for even though Takaaki was not the captain his hard work and physical power were highly regarded. If he'd stayed with the club his coach would see to it that he got into college somewhere on an athletic recommendation. But no matter how often the coach urged him to reconsider, Takaaki kept shaking his head. The coach refused to give up. He believed Takaaki was taking the incident too seriously and tried a different approach. "Look at it this way," he said. "All right, so you hit the referee, but that was just a sign of your youthful spirit. Now, if you were the sort of fellow who was always going around beating up people, it'd be a problem, but I can guarantee that that is not the case. Most colleges actually want kids with some fight in them, so this whole affair could work to your advantage." The coach talked until he had exhausted all argument. He knew that Takaaki was quiet and that he could be stubborn, but that he was so incredibly pigheaded was news to him. "So what are you going to do, then?" he asked. "Go to college," Takaaki replied. "And how do you think you'll manage that?" "By taking the entrance exams." The coach laughed. "You know how to play soccer, but that's about all you know. Not even a fifth-rate college will take you!" Takaaki turned his head away. Now the coach had had enough. "Fine! Do as you please!" Takaaki did. That same day he packed his bag and left.

Back in his Nippori boardinghouse, for the next three months Takaaki studied intensely for the entrance exams. He went to school only when he really could not avoid it, did not even allow himself time to take a bath or see people, and asked his landlady to put his meals on his desk. When he was tired, he rested his head on his books and took a nap. Most of his friends expected little from his effort. Since elementary school he had seldom opened a textbook, they said, so whatever he picked up this way was nothing more than a veneer of knowledge. It was going to be a disaster. When the results came in, he had failed six of the seven college entrance exams. With his beard, long hair, and unclipped nails, the Takaaki who went to check the notice board of his last hope—a mediocre private university—barely resembled the boy who had sported an ultra-short haircut since his first year in junior high. On the board he found his exam number on the list of successful candidates.

Shortly after his college entrance ceremony he received an invitation to join the official soccer club. He turned it down, though deep in his heart he still loved soccer. He was getting hopelessly out of shape now that he was spending endless hours in classrooms listening to lectures on such boring subjects as business administration. So he and a boy from Hiroshima he had met soon after his arrival formed their own club with a few friends. His leg had healed, and he was able to chase a ball again. Almost all members had joined the club for physical exercise, and some were rank beginners, but this motley crew did unexpectedly well. By summer they had won four straight matches against similar teams from other colleges, and that made them think seriously about participating in the local amateur league in the fall. They rented a room above a bar and had loud discussions about what to name their team and whether to use the Brazilian colors or Argentinean stripes for their uniform. They agreed on the name Red Devils—printed in English on uniforms of blazing crimson—and they finally decided to spend six days and five nights of their summer vacation training at the Echigo-Yuzawa hot springs, across the mountains north of Tokyo.

But during this training camp the club began to show signs of dissolution. Takaaki had been chosen captain because of his talent and experience, but some people felt that his training regimen was too rigorous, if not downright sadistic. It was no fun this way, one group complained, and another asked how they expected to compete in amateur league if they couldn't take the discipline here. The two groups refused to see eye to eye, and each night they argued in the presence of their brooding, silent captain. On the way to the hot springs there had been constant jokes and laughter; the trip back to Tokyo was silent and glum.

As it turned out, after their return to campus in the fall the Red Devils never got a chance to play soccer again. The year was 1968, and student riots were raging in the Japanese islands. Takaaki's university had its revolutionary groups, too, with their differently colored helmets and factions that fell apart between sunrise and sunset. These groups of young rebels had established their headquarters in the basement of the student union. Until that summer a clear line of demarcation had been drawn between them and other students, but when the administration tried to take advantage of the leaders' absence during the summer vacation by demolishing the union, the nonpolitical students felt their voices had not been heard, and their pent-up anger exploded. Riots spread like wildfire and soon engulfed the entire campus. Boys who until yesterday had wiled away their nights in mah-jongg parlors gathered in the university square brandishing weapons. Girls who had once skipped down campus lanes, their long hair trailing in the wind, tennis rackets in hand, were now carrying posters and shouting slogans about self-denial and resistance to authority.

The student union, already half demolished, was invaded again and, after some skirmishing, fell into student hands. But before they had time to bask in their victory they were besieged by riot police who cleared the building and arrested the ringleaders. The disorganized rebels could no longer offer effective resistance, and their struggle on campus collapsed. But this suppression only provoked the most sullen and embittered rebels to greater anger. The evil weed of authority was stretching its vicious roots beyond the universities toward all of society, and the rebels saw it as their duty to cut them off. Their watchword: revolution. Whenever they found a suitable target, they grabbed what weapons they could find and attacked. One of their number was Takaaki.

Protected by the sharp studs of his soccer shoes and a helmet he had stolen from a construction site, he roamed the field of battle, a makeshift weapon in hand. Takaaki insisted on the most violent action, and he incited his comrades with menacing rhetoric: "What the hell are you? A friend or an enemy? Prove it, or else!" At meetings he shouted radical dogma in a way that seemed infantile. Besieged by the jets of the water cannon or a mist of tear gas, he was conspicuous in his ferocity. Like a Shinto priest chanting incantations, he stood half-crouched, swinging his iron pipe, as he observed the foolish tactics of his foolish comrades who rushed unthinkingly at the serried shields confronting them, Takaaki searched for a weak spot in the enemy lines. He danced forward lightly as if he had measured the paces in advance, and with a couple of well-aimed blows opened a breach. The speed with which he escaped was astounding. They had to catch the demon, the men in blue decided, and they waited behind their strategically deployed shields, but time and again Takaaki coolly mocked their ineptitude. Raging over the merciless beating they had received, the men vented their frustrations on any students who had not escaped.

For a long time he hung out exclusively with comrades from the old Red Devils and kept the many leftist groups at a distance. But by 1970 the flames of campus unrest had slowly but surely burnt themselves out, so he and a handful of cronies joined one of the revolutionary factions. When asked why they wanted to join, they explained that in order to fight violence with violence they needed better weapons and organization and that the "army" of their choice had taken a clear position on these points. The young rebels were immediately accepted.

The name Revolutionary Army sounded glamorous, but the group was actually a pathetic band of eight or nine members. They operated underground, and the leaders were soon picked up and thrown in jail. The organization seemed doomed to extinction, but Takaaki and the other new members became the nucleus of the army. Their first priority was the acquisition of firearms, which they proposed to accomplish by robbing a weapons store outside Tokyo. The imprisoned leaders reacted with dismay: the authorities already had their eye on the organization, and it should keep a low profile.

Takaaki and his men refused. When asked how he intended to take responsibility if things went wrong under his leadership, he merely answered, "I will die." This provoked scathing comments: people who talked about nothing but dying were anachronisms, defeatists. A defeatist is someone who fears failure, he said, and is afraid to die. He dismissed all criticism as background noise. In silence he began to work on the execution of his plan.

After consulting only his closest advisers, Takaaki raided a weapons store in a small town in Ibaraki. The plan had been to break into the living quarters above the store late at night, tie up the owner and his wife, and steal rifles. Takaaki decided the victims—both elderly— would be too frightened to offer resistance, but he had underestimated the owner, who struggled so hard that the noise could be heard outside. And so instead of tying up the old man, Takaaki used his rope to strangle him.

The Revolutionary Army announced that it had won this battle and launched its next offensive, in which three more persons died. All three were former comrades who had broken off contact with headquarters and dropped out of sight after the murder of the weapons merchant. In the past they would have been reviled as opportunists, fair-weather revolutionaries, and that would have been it, but the deserters were a liability the organization could no longer ignore—they had to be executed. But if you are suddenly told you have to kill someone you used to kick a ball with, you feel trapped. There they sat, grinning crookedly, avoiding each other's eyes, until one of them spoke: all who had joined the Revolutionary Army had said they were willing to die, he declared, and therefore their former comrades had no choice but to die too, for deserters deserved death. This was strong language, and all heads jerked up, but to contradict was out of the question: the order had to be carried out.

Among the deserters was Takaaki's friend from Hiroshima with whom he had founded the Red Devils. Takaaki used to drop by his room almost every day and would often spend the night. Takaaki's familiarity with the location was the reason he was ordered to carry out the execution.

In the middle of the night Takaaki snuck into the apartment in Higashi-Nakano. After making certain the lights were out, he took the spare key his friend had given him. The door opened without resistance; the dark apartment smelled of coffee. His friend had always been proud of his Swiss coffeemaker: "You people never drink anything except instant. You've never tasted real coffee," he would say jokingly. Then his friend would play some jazz on his ridiculously large reel-to-reel tape recorder, grind some coffee by hand in his cast-iron coffee mill, and make a cup for everyone.

Takaaki did not bother to take off his shoes but stepped straight onto the wooden kitchen floor. He shifted his grip on the short iron pipe.

As always, he cast a glance at the poster on the sliding panel that separated the kitchen from the room—a carpet of bright-green grass and a soccer player sprinting magnificently after a ball—Pele in the 1970 World Championships in Mexico. Takaaki studied the poster briefly in the light from the window. Then he retied the towel he wore over his face and opened the door. From one of the beams of the low ceiling dangled a human body. His friend had hanged himself. Just as he realized what had happened, a putrid smell hit him in the face. Takaaki ran out of the apartment and into the night streets as if pursued by the devil.

On his lonely way home from the soccer stadium, amid the cool breeze, Manase at last realized what everyone else had understood long ago, that by entrusting Takaaki to his sister's care, he had rejected his son. His remaining duty to Takaaki was not especially onerous: tuition and living expenses, which he transferred to his son's account on the same day each month. Manase almost forgot what these automatic transactions were for. Learning of Takaaki's involvement in the radical student movement made no particular impression on him. Manase did not watch television or listen to the radio, or even subscribe to a newspaper. He had heard of a riot in the Yasuda Hall at Tokyo University, in a part of the city where he used to play as a child, but the news merely made him wonder what the neighborhood looked like now. He had only the vaguest idea what the student movement was or what it was trying to achieve. The public appeared to sympathize with the students, who bravely used stones and sticks to battle police units armed with steel and plastic; during the recruiting season, companies looking for signs of spirit actually preferred students who had been active in the movement. Having heard such reports, Manase saw no reason to worry. After some time he noticed his house was being watched by the police. When he told his sister, she hurried over, and her passionate defense of Takaaki eased his mind. She refused to believe it, she said, but if that boy had done anything illegal, he'd have done it for reasons very different from a common burglar—he'd have acted out of deep and logical conviction. Manase decided that at any rate he was no longer entitled to get involved, but if his son had wronged other people he was prepared to compensate for any damage or injuries, even if it meant selling everything he owned.

That was how Manase spent his days, untouched by the turmoil raging in the world. But then, without warning, just when he had convinced himself he would never see his son again, Takaaki appeared in the storehouse attic—on a windy December night, the longest of the year.

Manase had just taken an invigorating citron bath. He climbed up the ladder to the attic, switched on the lamp, and there, in front of him, sat his son.

"What are you doing here?" Manase asked. His words sounded like the lash of a whip. The moment he spoke he knew that was not the way to greet a son he had not seen in almost ten years. His blunder made him even more nervous. He did not know how to continue; his tongue uttered the opposite of what his heart felt. "As long as you haven't come for money," he heard himself say. He could have kicked himself.

Takaaki was sitting at a desk and did not seem offended by his father's reception. He'd only stopped by because he was in the neighborhood, he said, and when Manase heard the casual tone in which his son spoke, he was relieved.

"How about a cup of tea?" he asked as he put the kettle on the hot plate. "Or would you prefer a drink?" He remembered he still had a bottle of whisky someone had given him, but as soon as he stepped toward the ladder, he heard a sharp voice behind him: "Where are you going?" Manase was so surprised he almost fell down the hole, but he grabbed hold of the ladder. He saw Takaaki glaring at him through wide-open, terrifying eyes.

"I was only going to look for some whisky," was the father's dejected answer. Takaaki looked him over from head to foot, then suddenly the menace melted away.

"Tea's good enough," he said, smiling as if to make up for his outburst. But Manase caught the smell of blood, and he saw the face of a man whose eyes were swarming with maggots. He understood in a flash: Takaaki had killed someone. The words left his mouth in midthought: "You've killed someone, haven't you?"

Takaaki was dressed in flimsy khaki work pants and a lightweight jacket of the same color; his bare feet were in sandals and his thick neck muscles were visible under his close-cropped hair. He was picking up stones from a box on the desk, one by one, in the correct order. It was Hiroaki's collection of specimens which Manase had completed and then displayed on the desk. Even in death, the older brother had his own desk, while for the younger there was not even a place in his father's house. Manase worried that Takaaki might get angry when he realized how differently he had been treated, yet he felt as if Hiroaki's privacy was being invaded. But he stood still until Takaaki began to speak:

"And you never killed anyone during the war?" A thin smile played about his lips.

So that's it, thought Manase, as if agreeing with the logic of the question. He was so shocked by his son's implied admission of murder that his thoughts scattered like rats searching for a way out of a trap.

"Yes, but we're not at war now," he said lamely.

"Oh, but we are! And not only in Japan but in the entire world. You just haven't noticed."

The wind moaned around the storehouse. A tapping sound came from the lone cherry tree outside. It had been saved when the other trees around the house had been cut down, and its branches had grown in the shape of a spider's legs. Now the wind blew them against the attic window. Manase stopped listening to the sounds outside and concentrated at last on the reasons for his son's visit. What should he do? The first floor of the storehouse was probably safer than the attic. But the police had already been sniffing around his house earlier—it was too dangerous here. Should he hide somewhere deep in the mountains, or was it best after all to go to the police together, so Takaaki could give himself up peacefully? He rejected several plans. What use was geology to him now? Overwhelmed by a sense of futility and sadness, Manase could produce only the coldhearted question: "So what are you going to do now?"

"Oh, I'm prepared for the worst. I've been prepared from the beginning."

His son was going to die. He was dying already. He was speaking from the edge of the grave. Manase remembered the words Takaaki's mother had spoken long ago, seated here at this same desk: "Takaaki will die too." In his confusion he turned toward his son's distorted, grinning profile and uttered something entirely unexpected.

"But isn't the purpose of revolution to let people live? You don't start a revolution so they'll die, do you?"

Revolution. It was the first time the word

had crossed his lips. Takaaki glared at his cowering, deathly pale father with the same furious eyes and snorted contemptuously. Then he remarked, as if to avoid the issue, "I know this stone."

Manase noted that Takaaki was playing with one of the specimens from the box, but his thoughts lingered on the words he had just uttered. He answered absently: "Oh? That's very clever of you." He panicked again. It sounded as if he was making fun of Takaaki. Every time he opened his mouth he was sure to hurt him. He began to hate himself.

"It's chert. Green chert. Am I right?" Takaaki weighed the stone in the palm of his hand. It was indeed green chert. Besides, the name was written on the carton label stuck on the specimen.

"The average amateur doesn't see it that quickly, my boy. But...are you interested in stones?"

He was positive the opposite was the case, but the question escaped him anyway. This was the first time he had ever addressed Takaaki as "my boy," and he was not completely at ease with the phrase, but he did not know what else to call him. Takaaki did not answer but stared at the stone until Manase, who could no longer bear the silence, did something he knew was stupid: he launched into a long discourse on chert.

Chert is a sedimentary rock formed when the skeletons of Paleozoic organisms such as conodonts and radiolarians mixed with the silicic acid present in seawater; the green color is caused by ferrous oxidation. This specimen had been found in a bed that bordered on the lowest late-Silurian limestone stratum, which also contained a great number of chain corals as index fossils; this indicates that it was at any rate formed earlier, perhaps even as early as the middle of the Paleozoic era, which would make it one of the oldest formations in the Japanese isles. . . .

Takaaki now sat in the chair where for years Manase had seen the shade of Hiroaki—silent, his elbows on the desk, his eyes fixed on the stone in his hands. It was the same reverent posture Hiroaki assumed so often, and at that thought Manase could hold back no longer. He talked on and on, consoled by the spirit of his dead child, without considering Takaaki's reaction. Finally he reached the question that makes geology fascinating.

"Do you know, for instance, how rocks are

formed? Rocks are formed when red-hot magma cools off and solidifies into rock; rock erodes under the influence of wind and weather on the surface of the earth. That's how you get stones. Stones are eventually ground into sand, sand into soil; then stones and sand and soil are carried away by streams and settle on the bottom of lakes, fens, or the sea, where they once again harden into rock."

Manase could see the summer sun again, full and bright; a mountain brook sounded in his ears. He was absurdly showing off his erudition at a time like this—his son was a murderer on the run, and this explanation was the last thing he needed. Manase felt like weeping at his own futility, but he could no longer control himself. He began to wonder if these words had not been specially prepared for this moment. As Manase continued, his voice began to tremble with enthusiasm.

"In other words, the form of minerals is never static, not for a second; on the contrary, it undergoes constant change. All matter is part of an unending cycle. You know of course that even the continents actually move, though at an imperceptibly slow pace.

"What I'm trying to say is, the tiny pebble

that you might happen to pick up during a walk is a cross-section of a drama that began some five billion years ago, in a place that would later come to be called the solar system—a cloud of gas drifting idly through space, growing denser and denser until after countless eons it finally gave birth to this planet. That little pebble is a condensed history of the universe and keeps the eternal cycle of matter locked in its ephemeral form."

Manase heard a dry, nasty sound—a still, metallic rasp—that paralyzed him and made it impossible to continue. When he looked up, Takaaki was still at his desk, his Adam's apple bobbing up and down. Manase did not understand why Takaaki was laughing. Then he realized he was still standing over the floor opening—suspended, he thought. With an embarrassed smile he sat down in the nearest chair.

Takaaki looked up, the smile still on his lips. "Is that all you've learned in the past twenty, thirty years? I'm sorry, but I thought you'd been doing something much more impressive." When he laughed his clean-shaven face showed the same wrinkles in the corners of his eyes as his father; it seemed the only gentle thing about him. His narrow brow was sly and pointed, his chin stubborn; his thin, distorted lips betrayed indifference and cruelty. Manase tried to avert his glance from so much darkness, but he was mesmerized by Takaaki's motionless, deep-set eyes.

"Everybody knows that much. What you've just been telling me has been known for dozens of years. For a hundred yen I can buy a book and read the same stuff, that's what it all boils down to. You seem to think you're quite the scholar, but tell me, have you ever discovered anything new?"

Manase turned beet red. True, his contribution to science had been small indeed, his new theories were irrelevant. He wondered if he should mention the Paleoparadoxia, but all he'd really done was stumble over some animal bones. A child could have done the same thing.

After a short, sharp glance at his silent father, Takaaki resumed the attack. "In other words, all you've done in the past twenty, thirty years is not even worth a few hundred yen. It's as good as useless."

No! shouted Manase wordlessly. The feel of each separate stone in your hand. Its smell. Its taste. The mysterious colors and shapes of crystals and groundmass polished to a section. The miraculous accumulation of strata slumbering under the darkness of the forest, sculpted by water over millions of years. The breathing of minerals, noticeable only to those who venture alone and on foot into the deserted mountains. The order of the universe, unknowable until you have experienced it with all five senses. That wonder, that exhilaration, that awe, and more than anything, that endless sea of summer light—if only he could make his son see these things. But they were impossible to express in words. His eyes burnt with regret and sadness.

With a sidelong glance Takaaki observed his father weeping.

"Only someone who knows the essence of nature is a true scientist," Takaaki continued. "As long as you perceive the essence, the rest is not important. Fooling around with pebbles is not real science, that's all I want to say. If it makes you happy, fine, congratulations, but it's happy people like you that are making a mess of this world, with your indifference to what's essential. You're the ringleaders! But I didn't come here to criticize, I only wanted to ask you something."

Now that his emotional outburst had subsided, Manase became conscious of a cold trail of tears over his skin and a bitter taste in his mouth. The idea that he could influence his long-rejected son had been nothing but arrogance. He'd been a fool even to think about it. "What do you want to know?" he asked, but Takaaki said nothing and continued playing with the stone in his hand, as if wishing to savor his victory. Manase grew more dejected. This was his punishment for the selfish life he'd led, he thought. He cried.

As the night grew older the winter wind increased until it screamed in the distance with a force that made the mountains tremble. Manase was chilled to the bone. The oil stove was turned off, he noticed, but he did not have the energy to get up. The burning sensation of a few seconds ago had disappeared, and now his head felt as if he had fallen into a deep, dark hole. I wonder if the wind is blowing not only over the mountains, he thought absently, but also far away over the black sea.

The howling wind reminded Manase of the ship that had carried him to the Philippines. A few days (he forgot exactly how many) after leaving Sasebo, they had sailed through the center of a storm. The ship yawed and pitched until the soldiers, crammed in the stuffy hold like sardines in a tin, began to vomit. Unable to stand it any longer, Manase crawled up on deck and spent the rest of the night there. The deck was already packed—everyone had had the same idea—but somehow Manase managed to force himself into a tiny space. He laid his head on his arms—exposed to sudden showers and the flying spray of the waves, trembling with cold, sleepless with fear that they would sink—and listened to the shrieking of the wind.

"Did you ever go there?" Takaaki had emerged from his silence.

"Where?" Manase already knew the answer.

"The quarry where Hiroaki died. Did you go there?"

Manase shook his head, and once again Takaaki fixed his eyes on the stone in his hand.

"You know, I learned about green chert from Hiro. He told me just about everything there is to know about it."

The biting irony of a few minutes ago had disappeared, and Takaaki's somber voice warned Manase that he had come specifically to tell him this. The premonition of approaching doom made him forget the shock he had felt when he heard his son confess to murder. With fear in his eyes Manase stared at the stocky young man with the short hair.

"I was with Hiro, that day."

The smell of burnt limestone hit Manase's nostrils—the shadeless, straw-colored landscape of the quarry, the dazzling reflection of the sun, and the deafening chirping of cicadas. Through the rising waves of hot air the dark forest trembles. On the white rock floor Manase saw two small dark specks, two boys in shirts and short pants who park their bicycles in the stone arena and walk toward the high cliff—the very embodiment of danger. In the tall grass at the end of the cliff they find the yawning black mouth of the cave and they peer silently inside. Then, one after the other, the darkness swallows them up.

"I held the flashlight, and Hiro tapped on the walls with his hammer."

The sound of the hammer causes an amazingly loud echo. If you beat on the walls of a cave with a hammer you run the risk of a cave-in. But the two boys do not know that, so you cannot expect them to be that careful. The big brother holds a stone in his open hand and shows his little brother what he has found. This is green chert, he explains. It is a kind of rock from skeletons of ancient organisms that have hardened together with silicic acid, and the green is iron oxide. The big brother explains it in exactly the same words he heard his father use, then he proposes exploring a bit farther because there are bound to be good fossils here. Slowly the two boys penetrate deeper into the cave. Soon their way is barred by a worn old fence. They shine their flashlight on a crack between the planks and stare silently inside.

"And then we heard a voice. Or rather, I thought I heard something, but Hiro said he was certain. There was somebody in there, he said."

In the rotting fence the children easily made an opening large enough for them to crawl through. Careful, maybe it's a dangerous animal! The little brother tries to stop him, but the big brother, certain he has heard a human voice, goes to take a look, saying he'll be back. He slips through the hole and disappears into the depths of the cave. The little brother stays behind and clings to the fence. He tries to pierce the darkness with his eyes. Soon the light of the torch disappears. Left alone in the dark, the little boy can no longer conquer his fear and calls out for his brother—first crying, then screaming—until the echoes sound through the entire cave.

"But no matter how long I waited, he didn't come back. He didn't answer, either. I was so frightened, I had no idea what to do. I only knew I wanted to be with him. So I crawled through the fence too."

The kettle whistled on the hot plate. Takaaki fell silent, languidly turned his head, and stared at the steam. He looked as if he had never seen anything so strange. Manase felt seasick, and a sour liquid pushed up against the bottom of his throat. By swallowing his saliva he managed to control it, but he checked to see if the empty bucket was still at his feet.

"I have no idea what happened. Absolutely no idea."

Takaaki's eyes seemed shrunken.

"The next thing I remember I was outside."

All alone in the sun-baked limestone arena sits a little boy. The forest, now wrapped in even blacker hues, lifts its expressionless face toward the child. Slowly the sunlight becomes saturated with shadows; once the blood-red sun dips below the mountain rim, dusk will come swiftly. The child has been drawing figures on the ground with a twig, but when he sees that the black shadow of the cliff is about to swallow him, he looks up and stares anxiously about him.

Then he runs to his bike and, his tiny buttocks lifted off the seat, pedals as fast as he can down the gravel road, until he disappears behind the hills in the distance.

"I was wondering what could have happened to Hiro, and then I suddenly got scared and hurried home. My head ached so badly that Mama thought I had sun poisoning and put me to bed. I fell asleep instantly. In the middle of the night I woke up and learned what all the commotion was about, but Hiro had warned me not to tell a soul how we'd gone into the mountains together. If I let on, I'd really be in trouble, I thought, so I pulled the blanket over my head and lay there, trembling. Mama must have noticed something, for she questioned me fiercely. Why did I leave Hiro and go home by myself? What happened after I crawled through that hole in the fence? I was so little, I don't remember much. You weren't home that day, were you?"

"No, I was away. That day I was away."

Manase glanced at the face of the man at the desk, but it showed virtually no expression.

"But there is one thing that I remember very well."

Takaaki's voice betrayed his nostalgia for the

past but at the same time it sounded cool and neutral, the voice of someone who has come to report the facts. And yet, Manase thought he seemed to hear an almost imperceptible quiver in that voice. What is it? he wanted to ask. What do you remember? But the words refused to come out. Takaaki continued.

"Blood. There was blood on my hands. I noticed when I rode away on my bike. When I got home, I tried desperately to wash it off."

"It can't have been you!" shouted Manase, his heart thumping in time with his son's fear as soon as he heard the word "blood."

"In the first place you didn't carry a knife. And secondly, a child could never have done such a thing. It was sap. It must have been sap. There are lots of lacquer trees in that forest, and you got the sap on your hands. That's what you must have thought was blood!"

"Oh, I don't think I did it."

Takaaki's voice was flat—it showed no sign of suspicion, no trace of sarcasm, and that brought his father back from the edge of panic. Manase stared imploringly at his son's face.

"I didn't have a reason, did I? I admired my brother, I loved him. But I still can't help wondering what really happened that day. It gives me no peace. They never caught the man who did it, did they?"

Manase nodded. A blue-black shadow sank over the cold, tired, blank face that Takaaki turned to his father, but the outlines of the face he had had as a child floated to the surface. The armor of his eternal grin had been abandoned; this was the face he wore when alone. For the first time Manase felt that he was seeing the son he used to know. If only I could call him by his name, he thought from the bottom of his heart. And not just that. There is still so much I want to do for him. But what could he do? The kettle whistled vainly on the hot plate. Pull the plug—that was all.

In the brief silence, Takaaki fondled the green chert specimen again, and with the same reverence. "I'm taking this with me," he said. He put it in the pocket of his jacket and got up.

"Why don't you stay here tonight?" Manase asked, flustered and urged on by a voice that ordered him not to let Takaaki go. "I never even gave you your tea. And didn't you want to ask me something?" Outside, the storm raged in the night. Manase wanted to stop his son, but the way Takaaki stood there with both feet planted on the floor made him seem twice as big as his father—so strong and swift that he needed only to give him a tiny push to bounce him ten, fifteen feet away. Manase was powerless against this impression of physical strength. Takaaki's tense, lonely shoulders and back, his stubborn neck muscles—the only spot of his body where he had a tiny roll of fat, like a middle-aged man—rebuffed his father's invitation, refusing even to recognize his existence. His son had come without notice, so it was natural he should leave without saying good-bye, thought Manase. Takaaki already had one foot on the ladder. Manase stood up, his mind blank, helpless and with a feeling of unfathomable weakness in his cold, aching knees, and watched his son descend.

"What I meant to ask is . . . Oh, well, it's really ridiculous." Only Takaaki's head was still visible in the floor opening. He was laughing. "When we heard that voice from the back of the cave, Hiro said it was yours. 'That's Daddy's voice,' he said. But of course you weren't there that day. Were you?"

After the holdup of the weapons store Takaaki and his comrades disappeared until the middle of winter. They surfaced in Asahikawa in northern Hokkaido, where they attacked a police station in the center of town. The idea was to walk in one evening as if to ask for directions, catch the policemen off guard, and steal their revolvers. They had rehearsed the plan many times, but at the critical moment somebody walked into the station—to ask for directions. One member of the group panicked and started waving his weapon. The officers drew their guns. The rest of the group were waiting in the getaway car, and when they saw what was happening they ran inside and started shooting. Takaaki took a bullet in the thigh. He managed to drag himself to the car, but just when he had begun to fire random salvos at the police station with a shotgun, the northern night resounded with such a howling of sirens that it seemed as if every patrol car in Japan was gathering here. The assailants tried to escape by abandoning their car and fleeing into the busy city traffic, but by midnight they had all been picked up. Takaaki resisted to the last. Under a thin, waning moon he was finally cornered behind an old lumberyard in an open field overgrown with weeds. After using all his cartridges, he charged out, swinging his shotgun as if it were a club. He was shot dead.

By the time the news reached him Manase had already made his decision. A dark rage had finally given the indecisive, almost pathologically timid owner of the storehouse the impetus he needed to act. The person who has driven my wife insane and sent my two children to their death is none other than me. Once that unshakable conviction had crystallized in his heart, he directed his anger at himself and at a mysterious black shadow standing behind him and keeping his body locked in an unrelenting embrace. He would have been unable to give it a name, and when he tried to get a better view of it, his heart shrank with fear. Manase thought of the pain Hiroaki must have suffered in that dark cave, and about the sadness that had driven Takaaki to seek his own death amidst loneliness. Manase snorted through his nose, briefly and sharply like an excited billy goat, to encourage himself.

Manase sold his bookstore cheaply and spent his days and nights in his attic. At the suggestion of an acquaintance, he had been working on a book called *Stone Collecting in Chichibu*. This was a handbook for beginners, about two hundred pages long, in which he described the strata and geological features of the

Chichibu area and explained how to start a stone collection. Because it would contain everything he had learned in his career as a self-taught geologist, he gave it all his attention and energy. He organized the materials he had collected over the years and began, at first hesitantly, to fill page after blank page with characters.

Winter passed; the cherry blossoms outside his attic window bloomed and fell; the limestone mountains glittered at their whitest; and still he wrote on. August was running its course and the anniversary of Hiroaki's death was near. For three days he worked without rest; finally, as the lusty crowing of the neighbor's rooster announced a new dawn, Manase finished his last page. The day had come.

He stuffed his completed manuscript into an envelope and was about to address a label to the professor in Kyoto who had first advised him to publish his work, when he had second thoughts. Finishing the manuscript had given him such a tremendous sense of satisfaction that he no longer found it necessary to have it published. He took it out of the envelope and wrote under the title: "For my wife and my two sons." He put the manuscript in a drawer and fell asleep in his chair.

For the first time in years Manase had a dream that was not a nightmare: the storehouse, surrounded by the luxuriant foliage of the ancient trees; the beds of sweet yams his sisters cultivated in the garden; the mountains seen from the bridge across the Arakawa; the deep strata under the green forest along the Yokose—one by one these scenes floated through his mind, in gold-rimmed clear images, with no human beings in sight. It was neither lonely nor sad.

Manase opened his eyes with the fulfillment deep sleep usually brings. It was past five already, and because he had wanted to finish everything while there was still daylight, he had a quick bite to eat and prepared to go out. He changed into his field clothes and once more picked up the specimens on Hiroaki's desk. Thirty pieces of rock in an old cookie box. Except there were only twenty-nine now. Since last winter one square had been empty. Manase's intention was to finish the set once more, but this time the missing piece, green chert, could only come from one place—the cave.

In the attic his equipment and specimens lingered silently in the twilight. Manase cast one last glance around the rapidly darkening room and climbed down the ladder.

He pedaled fast, but it was night when he reached his destination; stars were visible in the narrow sky between the mountaintops. The old gravel road was paved now, and there were so many new houses that during the last half of his ride he began to worry that the cave might have disappeared. But in the darkness the quarry cliff soared just as high as before. When he forced his way through the bushes, with the chirping of insects in his ears, the entrance was where he remembered it to be.

The wooden cover was rotting away, and the barbed wire was so rusty he did not need his wire cutter. One kick with the heel of his shoe was enough. He crawled through the opening and proceeded to the back of the cave until he reached the partition barring further progress. There he switched off his flashlight and peered through a crack between the planks.

He saw—a light. "So I was right," Manase whispered. He nodded a few times with short, sharp jerks of his head. By sighing deeply two or three times he managed to keep his breathing under control. Seeing the flickering light with his own eyes, he realized the significance of the decision he had made the past winter. To penetrate to the back of the cave. To conquer his fear and walk on. To do what he must do: confront the thing waiting for him at the back of the cave.

He hesitated, debating whether to collect his chert now or later; he decided he could do it on his way back—if there was a way back. He felt a sudden stirring of fear, but it melted away in the embers of his anger, which he stoked into a blazing fire by imagining, one by one, the faces of his dead sons.

Manase removed a plank and noted with satisfaction that his hands were not trembling. He had crept through the narrow opening, past the partition, and got to his feet. A current of wet, warm air stroked his cheeks. Fixing his eyes on the campfire, he noticed that the layer of green chert continued into this part of the cave. He congratulated himself on his composure as he coolly observed every single thing around him, and he was about to study the strata more closely when he realized he had left his flashlight on the other side of the partition. This first small error upset him, breaching the dam of his self-possession. But the moment he turned to run back, he was blinded by the flashing of a naked blade. He felt the shadows on the rock wall slowly crawling toward him. The fear he thought he had locked up in its cage buried its claws deep inside him. A sharp voice shouted: "Manase! Manase!" His determination and anger melted. In his place stood a soldier waiting motionless, like a wooden statue, for his orders.

"Damn this bloody noise! It's keeping everyone awake! Manase, go kill him!"

It was inevitable. Everything he did was inevitable. With the piercing voice ringing in his ears, Manase accepted the sword offered by the man with the smile under the shadow of his cap. He bent over the dying man on his bed of rock. He took the sword in his left hand and opened the rags of the uniform, baring the man's chest. The neck looked like a chicken leg. Kill him, Manase! See if you can do it, Manase! Encouragement fell over his back; he slowly extended the sword toward its target. That's right, that's the way to do it, don't mess things up now, pull it around lightly, as if you're cutting through water. Now cut! Nice and easy! Goaded by the indefatigable, seductive voice resonating inside his head, Manase placed the sword tip on the soldier's grimy, desiccated skin. At that moment, the dying man opened his eyes.

"Can't you let me live until I've seen the sun one more time?"

Even as the lance corporal uttered these words, the shadows swelled behind the soldier with the sword in his hand until they engulfed his body. For one second his heart had been moved by this last, pathetic wish. Manase had to laugh at the coward begging for his life at a time like this. See the sun one more time? No way. They would all die in this dark cave. They were all dead already. This darkness was death itself. And only those who could bear this eternal darkness were able to control death. Conquer death. He would show them how well he could cut. Swiftly, gracefully. With his own two hands he would see what death felt like. To prove that he was among those who did not fear it.

The lance corporal whispered on, but Manase was no longer listening. He cleansed his heart of evil thoughts and fixed his eyes on the black veins in the dying man's neck. Silently he recited the correct way to kill a human being with a sword and his heart overflowed with confidence. He smiled and suddenly noticed how strangely the man lay there, with both hands pressed against his chest. In the palms of his hands he was holding a small gray stone. Even as Manase pondered what kind of amulet it was, the words reached his ears:

"Even the most ordinary pebble has the history of the universe written on it."

The shadows in the cave writhed wildly. From behind came a voice that lashed his body. "Kill him! Kill him! Kill him!" Like someone fighting against a roiling torrent he planted both feet on the earth and resisted the forces pushing him.

"This green chert, for instance, consists of the petrified bones of ancient organisms. One day, our bones will be like this. This is how the dead come to life again."

The lance corporal continued. "Hornblende-gabbro, quartz-diorite, variolite, olivine basalt." Manase slowly realized that these strange, abstract-sounding words were the names of stones, and he repeated: "Hornblende-gabbro, quartz-diorite, variolite, olivine basalt." As he pronounced each name, he felt the stone in his hand. The centipedes began to squirm on the walls and the shadows writhed ever wilder: the person at the fire had stood up. In the bright red light of the flames, the straw-colored uniform moved toward him, leaning on the sheath of the sword, like a three-legged monster.

Manase flung the sword away. The echoes clanged through the hollows of the cave, and by the time they died down he had grabbed the prostrate man by the arms and pulled him to his feet. Manase dashed headlong for the entrance, with the lance corporal on his back. As he jumped outside he saw in a flash an image that remained etched on his retina: a crouching figure within picking up the sword, a featureless face in the shadow of the cap. Without looking back Manase fled into the darkness of the jungle with its scent of trees and grass—slipping and sliding down the steep slope of the gorge toward a place with water, his skin rent by the hard leaves.

The descent took so incredibly long it felt as if he were working his way down the rim of a bottomless bowl, but as time passed he began to feel safer. The moment he decided he was out of danger, he began to tremble like a leaf, his knees gave way, and he sank into the grass. Then, at last, from deep in the darkness, he heard the murmur of water. After a brief rest he continued cautiously. At the bottom of the gorge, under the starlight through the trees, he saw a black river. He lowered his burden—who now felt as light as decayed wood—from his shoulders and laid him on the ground. Manase cupped some water in his hands and, after drinking a little himself, offered some to the corporal.

The lance corporal took a small sip and continued his story. About the long, long history of the earth. About the mysterious structure of the universe. The words Manase heard as he lay in the soft grass were spoken by a human being and offered incontestable proof that he was still alive. Sighing deeply, he listened as the words quietly melded with the singing of the stream.

In the sky above them floated myriad heavenly bodies. Manase's eyes climbed higher and higher, far above the mountains, through the firmament, to the most distant corner of the universe. From that infinitely remote spot in the unknown, Manase looked down upon himself, a tiny figure in the nook of an enormous vessel.

Dawn. In the white, misty forest the sound of chattering birds and monkeys was everywhere. The jungle was returning to life. The sun was not yet visible, but the lance corporal lifted his eyes to the gold-rimmed mountains, smiled, and extended the stone in his hand to Manase.

"This is what the children gave me. The two children that came to the cave.... They gave it to me."

The lance corporal closed his eyes. Manase moistened his lips with a cloth he had dipped in the river and folded the dead man's hands over his chest.

Suddenly the river was bathed in a transparent light. The pebbles on its bottom assumed the brightest hues. Manase looked at the stone he held in his fingers. An ordinary, gray stone... But the moment he took the wet cloth to wipe it clean, the sun rose over the mountains, and in his hands the stone was changed into a radiant crystal.

Breinigsville, PA USA
18 July 2010
242013BV00003B/9/P